To Vera

Thank You! Yours my first sale please let me have feedback
I'd love to know what you think

ADVENTURES IN MAGIC

Rebecca Janzen

Rebecca Janzen

 **FriesenPress**

Suite 300 – 990 Fort Street
Victoria, BC, Canada V8V 3K2
www.friesenpress.com

ISBN

978-1-4602-5076-1 (Hardcover)
978-1-4602-5077-8 (Paperback)
978-1-4602-5078-5 (eBook)

1. Juvenile Fiction, Science Fiction, Fantasy, Magic

Distributed to the trade by The Ingram Book Company

THIS BOOK IS DEDICATED TO MY own pack, to my family thank you for always believing in me even when I didn't believe in myself. This is especially for my mother my editor. Thanks mum.

ACKNOWLEDGEMENTS

H I ALL BELIEVE IT OR NOT this feels like its harder to write then the story itself. So lets start with the obvious. Thank you for picking up my book and giving it a chance to drag you in. I'd like to thank my mother who acted as my editor and charged me nothing. I'd also like to thank FriesenPress for having patience with me and giving me this opportunity. I want to say something inspirational here unfortunately I've got nothing. I would also like to thank all the great writers I've read over the years for teaching me you are only limited by your imagination. Jules Vern, H.G Wells, Frank Herbert, Angie Sage, Diane Duane, Roald Dahl, Marianne Curley, Garth Nix, Paul Stewart & Chris Riddell, David and Leigh Eddings, Terry Goodkind and Derek Landy to name a few without these great authors to inspire me to reach for my goals I'd probably still be sitting quietly in my room instead I'm reaching for the moon and hopping to land among the stars I admire. Guess I did manage something inspirational after all so all you young writers like me reach for the moon see you in the stars. Don't be afraid to let others read your work or ask for help you never know where you'll wind up. Most of all though don't be afraid to reach out to authors you admire. Even if all they send back is a thank you it means as much to them as you. Anyway sit back and enjoy the ride the stories about to begin so hold onto your hats tie up your laces and get ready!

PART 1
THE COST OF LIFE

CHAPTER 1

CALL OF THE FOREST

THE SUN SHONE BRIGHTLY AS IT rose over a beautiful spring day. Most days were either far too hot or a mass of never ending storms. The weather had become bizarre in the last decade. The winters were no longer as they had been with massive snowfalls. They were quickly becoming a fairytale parents told to their children. Enough snow to sled on in winter and cool summer days. The constant storms or sweltering temperatures were all the little ones knew about. This world has many tales to be told, as tapestry has many strings. This tale is one of those strands part of a greater picture. One wrong string though, could destroy the entire picture.

The scent of wood smoke smouldering hung heavy in the air of an ordinary bedroom. The room is occupied by a girl of sixteen. The girl sneezes in her sleep. The smoky smell became stronger and stronger until the air itself smoked. This was not a regular smoke. The smoke was somehow contained in a small ball. As time went by, a flame appeared within the ball of smoke. The flame spread, turning the ball of smoke red. From the remains of last night's fire came a red bird. The bird flew over, landing on the girls dresser. The bird turned itself into a piece of paper which folded in half as it came to rest on her dresser.

Tempest rolled from her bed sneezing. The fire and smoke were gone. Tempest looked around questioningly, "It must have been a dream." Walking over to her dresser she got dressed in her usual clothes, cargo pants and a light green tie-die t-shirt. Tempest looked at her dresser, she was not the neatest person in the world, but she knew that folded paper hadn't been there last night. She picked up the note and unfolded it. "Urgent, please come to Fern Park. Be there by 7:30am." Tempest looked around her room trying to figure out how the note had gotten there. Her parents wouldn't have put it there. She could hear their snores emanating from the basement.

Tempest looked around her room. It was her normal mess. Her bed looked more like a nest. The blankets formed walls around the centre sleeping pit. Her computer, which sat on her desk, and her dresser. It was a normal teenagers room: roller blades, video games, art supplies and books, hundreds of books. Glancing at her watch, she made her way to the kitchen. If she hurried she would just have time for a bite of breakfast.

Tempest sat down at the table. Toast and cereal for breakfast, simple. Breakfast done, she left the house. Her bike was behind the garage and she dragged it through the gardens, hopping her dad wouldn't notice the damage to his precious flowers. The park was a ten minute ride and she had eight minutes to spare, a challenge, lovely. It was shaping up to be an interesting day. The note was strange and Tempest felt compelled to do as it requested.

Fern Park was a straight downhill ride, if you coasted it took ten to twelve minutes. She would be late if she took it easy. Speed was the order of the day. Tempest skidded to a halt at the entrance to Fern Park, 7:30 on the dot. First challenge met and won. She got off her bike and locked it into the bike rack. There was a hill at the park, large enough to be an awesome sledding hill for any child. Now though, it was barren ground. The grass had been burnt away in last year's heat wave.

Meanwhile, a teenage boy, lay in the tall burnt grasses at the top of the hill watching the girl he had left the note for slowly approach. Her blond hair shone in the sunshine. Bright blue-grey eyes looked up toward where he lay. Tempest Rainstorm was right on time. She had to be the one who could save his people, if his information was correct.

Tempest shook her head as she walked past where the old metal playground had once stood. It was sad to see it so empty. The slide and climbing cage that gave burns from the hot sun had long been taken away. The city had replaced the metal with plastic. Safer equipment installed giving less of a thrill at conquering. The tennis courts still stood, as did the old trees. The hill stood grandly in front of the woods. Tempest knew that the best view of the area was from up top of the hill. The only sound to be heard was the cawing of seagulls and new leaves rustling on the trees before summer came to burn them away. Walking to the top of the hill, the woods stared back at her. Nothing seemed out of place. Where was the person who left the note? She sat down on the hill and waited. It was past seven-thirty by ten minutes according to her phone. Tempest stood up and yelled, "I'm here. What do you want?" Watching the trees for a response, waiting with the wind blowing and the birds screeching.

"Hello Tempest," said a voice behind her. Jason's deep voice echoed. Tempest turned around, fist up and ready to fight. Within two feet of where she stood was a boy who looked barely older than she was. Bright green eyes bore into her own. He wore cut off jeans, and that was it. No shirt, no shoes. His black spiked hair blew in the wind. Tempest watched his face as a mischievous grin danced across his face, a half smile seemed permanently fixed to his face.

"Who are you and how do you know my name?" Tempest took a step back trying to put some distance between them. The boy smirked, watching her like she was an interesting bug he had found under a rock. She rolled her shoulders, cracking her neck. She hated being observed.

"I'm Jason. I know you because I sent you that letter." Trying to catch him unaware, Tempest leapt forwards attacking him. "How did you get into my bedroom?" Tempest shoved him backwards. She knocked him to the ground, her fist inches from his face. Jason simply laughed at her. Hoping to scare an answer from his lips, she slammed her first forward hitting the ground. Her fist should have hit next to his head, but for some reason the space was already empty. Her fist forming the crater where she hit the barely moist ground.

Jason stood before her grinning as he brushed himself off. "I'll tell you if you stop trying to hit me, or did you want to try tenderizing the ground again?" A half smile lit his face. His eyebrows twitched with amusement. Tempest stood, looking at him warily, as though watching a wild animal. "How'd you do that?" She blinked and sputtered a few times trying to figure out how he moved so fast. Jason laughed again, "Speed is relative."

"Well, if you aren't going to tell me how you moved, then how did you get the note into my room?" Jason snapped his fingers and a flame appeared above his hand. "A spell, magic, nothing complex." Tempest shook her head, a few pieces of hair falling from her pony tail into her face. She tucked the loose strands behind her ear. "Magic is only an illusion." As Jason shook his head in the negative and let out a heavy sigh, she blurted out, "It is I was an amateur magician."

"Magic is imagination. If you believe it and can describe it, it becomes possible. What are words but descriptions for things you believe?" Tempest blinked slowly, watching Jason carefully. Maybe this guy was crazy and dangerous. Jason sighed, she lacked understanding. What did he expect? She knew nothing of magic, real magic. She had grown up in a world of technology. Suddenly, he laughed. "I'm so glad you decided to come. I need your help. We, you and me, are going to save magic and perhaps even fix your human world a little."

Tempest took a step back. "What do you mean fix my world? What's wrong with it? What is this some kind of crazy quest?" Stammering and backing away, he was definitely a crazy person. Magic and quests only existed in books or video games not in the real world. Reaching the edge of the hill she leapt. It wasn't a straight drop. There were smaller hills on the back of the hill. Not hills really, just rocks to slow you down. Tempest continued down and ran for the forest, desperate to escape the crazy guy. It had been a mistake to come here. She glanced back to be sure he wasn't following her and SMASH. What had she run into? There had been a clear path. Tempest looked up. Jason rubbed his chest, she had run straight into him. Definitely, not an illusion. How had he gotten ahead of her? Jason cocked his head to one side, "Wanna, try that again?" He was trying hard not to laugh, which did nothing to help her pride. He offered her his hand and pulled her up to stand beside him.

Nervously, Tempest pulled out her phone looking for reception. No bars. That had never happened in the city. She thought about running again, she didn't think that would work. "No, I think you proved I can't out run you." Tempest continued to try and get her phone to work. She had to call her parents, hoping to get help. "Your phone won't work here. When you entered the forest you entered the magic world. Magic needs you so you are locked in. You are outside your time here. When we fix magic, then you will be free to return to the human world, if you wish. If you try to leave before we complete our 'quest,' as you put it, the magic will stop you. Jason had a very smug look on his face. She was trapped.

"Prove it!" Tempest walked back the way they had come. Jason followed her. There was a field at the edge of the woods. But try as she might she couldn't step out of the forest. It was as though there was a wall in front of her. "How did you get out?" Tempest demanded. She looked around carefully, the leaves were frozen in the breeze. Her eyes hunted for a trace of movement. She watched the leaves, willing them to move. Birds were frozen in mid flight…

"Magic. But now I can no more pass through the barrier than can you. When we fix magic, you will be able to walk through with ease. You see, the magic world is currently in trouble. This is an emergency barrier…No one in-no one out."

The birds frozen in mid flap were really starting to freak her out. Gravity should have come into effect, causing them to fall to earth. There were the trees stone still and plants unmoving in the wind. What had happened to the wind? There was always a breeze. "So, time has stopped?" Shaking her head slowly, impossible is what this is, was the only thought in her head. The world was frozen. Not from cold but from time.

Jason nodded. "Now, will you listen to me?" He watched her as though expecting her to bolt again. She sighed and nodded slowly. He let out a sigh of relief. "I'm sorry I resorted to chasing you. If I could do this without a human I would. You are one of the few humans that carry the magic gene within this city. It was logical to ask you to help."

"I guess I have no choice now do I?" Jason nodded and walked away from her, expecting her to follow. It was either stay stuck at the forest edge or follow him and find a way out. No choice really. Tempest jogged to keep up to Jason. His head brushed against the lowest branches. Tempest stood on tippy toe and tried to reach the branches with her hand. No luck. How tall must he be? Six foot ten at least. "Can you slow down? Your legs are longer than mine." Jason slowed down enough for her to walk beside him instead of jogging. "Are all humans as short as you?" Tempest glared up at him. If she hadn't already tried to leave the woods she would have right then. Unfortunately, leaving wasn't an option. Trapped in a forest with a crazy man. Her mom was right, she did run without looking where she was going. If she got out of this mess, her mom was getting an apology.

Walking further and further from the world she knew curiosity got the better of her. "Where are we going anyway?" Tempest tripped on the tree branches and roots on the forest floor. How did Jason move so easily, yet she was tripping on everything? "We are going to my home. You need to be prepared for what we are going to do. You have to prove yourself to my pack. It will help you to understand what we are fighting for." He watched as she tripped again and caught her hand. Jason guessed it was time he started to teach her. He showed her how to read the forest path. To look where the path lay hidden from view. Nodding slowly, Tempest asked. "So, at this place, there is at least going to be some decent food right?" Her stomach had started to grumble loudly. Whenever she was nervous, she got hungry. Tempest opened her backpack and pulled out a water bottle. She drank slowly. Who knew when she would find fresh water or food.

Jason let out a laugh. "There will be food, we do eat well at my camp. My home is one of the oldest settlements. We are a traveling clan and this is our summer camp. In the winter we travel to Emor. Emor is filled with every kind of creature imaginable, dragons, centaurs, dwarves and fairies. Emor is a magnificent city. When the sun hits the AMS, the Advanced Magic School, at the right angle, it shoots rainbows. It rains every hour. The flight tower is a giant tree where the hatcheries are located. The city of the dwarfs is so deep underground you'd think they were next to the core. Warm, safe and lava art decorates their caverns. Lava art is so amazing. It's always moving and changing colours. The fairy glades are wonderful. Sparkling and showy with light-dance and music-trees. Rainbow rivers...it's a city of peace." Jason's voice trailed off quietly.

Tempest listened as Jason wove a description of magnificent structures made of both trees and stone. He must be crazy, Tempest thought. He really seems to believe in all these fairy tale creatures. Jason continued to speak of underground cities and towers of gryphon hatcheries. Tempest let out a small sigh. It would indeed be a wonderful place if it was real. Jason smiled as he spoke, his eyes half closed as though he could see the city. "If we succeed in our quest, I could show you."

"IF, what do you mean IF we succeed? What if we don't?" Jason turned back when he reached the top of the hill they were walking up.

He watched her through the tree branches. "I won't lie to you. We are the fifth team. The other four teams were killed. That could happen to us. It's always a possibility on a quest." He walked back towards her. "I'm sorry. You don't know how important this is to magic. If there was any other way I wouldn't have come to you."

Tempest looked at him and noticed how green his eyes were. He had no pupils, just solid green with an occasional flash of red across where the pupil was supposed to be. "What's with your eyes?" Jason walked away motioning her to follow, "When we get to camp you'll see." They walked for an hour or more in silence before they came upon a clearing. Littered throughout the clearing were tents and huts. A huge log house and a modern washroom build, just like the ones at the city pool, lay near the middle of the clearing. Adults stood talking or working going about their daily lives. Everyone was dressed the same, in hiking boots, hats, cotton t-shirts and like Jason with only pants on. Tempest's eyebrows raised up in question, "This is your camp?" Jason grinned and nodded. He lead her down to the people. Down through the camp, until they reached a small hut. The hut was formed by four pillars holding up a roof. The walls were curtains attached to the pillars. One of the curtains was tied back revealing kids and an elderly woman with grey hair. She was tall, like Jason. Behind her, inside the hut, was a statue. Tempest felt a flash of recognition at seeing the statue. It was a statue of Romulus, Remus and their wolf Lupa. That seemed strange to find here in a mobile summer camp.

Jason's grin got bigger. "That's my mom, Jessica. The kids are the first year initiates. When the spring solstice comes in a few days, they will attempt to become adults and join the pack. Most have already been changing for a couple of years but haven't gained complete control." He crouched down and rested on his haunches listening to his mother. Tempest wondered what in the world he meant by "the change" but followed his example and sat quietly beside him.

Jessica was in the middle of a lesson. "Werewolves are important to magic. We are the balance keepers. We are one of he few species which can use every type of magic. There is no need for us to beg the elements to work for us, they simply do. We are the only shape changers left. Most of all, we are one of the few species who raise our young and belong to a pack all our lives. No matter where we travel, we always have a home. Within the pack, we always have family." She picked up a piece of straw, breaking it in half. "Just as this straw, we break if alone. But, together we are strong." She picked up a few more pieces and tried to break them again. This time they didn't break. She smiled at the kids. This solstice, you will try to join us as part of this living force. You have undergone training. With the others that are facing the trials you will try for the first time. You will run separately but you will have your chance." She smiled, "Go on, go play with your pack mates, I have to teach the basics to a newcomer." The kids sprang up happy to be dismissed. Tempest briefly wondered if she was also dismissed before realizing she was the newcomer.

Jason smiled as they stood up and he introduced Tempest to his mum. "Tempest this is my mother, Jessica, she is one of the pack leaders. Mum, this is Tempest." He didn't elaborate, apparently, her name said it all. "So nice to meet you Tempest." She turned to Jason and

continued. "Cutting it a bit close Jason? We have an hour before the first trial." Jessica turned back towards Tempest and continued gruffly. "This is our mother, the wolf mother, Lupa. Lupa guides and protects the pack. Werewolves are almost as old as elves and older than vampires, though they will say otherwise. The four solstices are important to us. They are what allow our cubs to join the pack. Those who want to enter the training, and those who attempt the trials do so at the solstice. The cubs who don't pass the trials enjoy another couple of months as children. Those that pass are given more responsibilities. They are taught what it means to be an adult. How to take care of the pack." Tempest could tell she was just getting the barebones of life here in the pack, but she didn't mind. She was having a very hard time coming to terms with this new world and the fact that all her childhood fairy tales were true. This world was so close to one of her childhood haunts, Fern Park. How had she missed finding it?

Tempest had noticed Jason's eyes earlier. Now, she looked around and saw that he was the only one, everyone else had deep red eyes. She nodded trying to take in all the information she had been given. "Why are Jason's eyes so green and everyone else's are red with bits of green?" Elves, vampires and werewolves? What were these next to the fact that Jason had done real magic?

Jessica smiled, "You see much for one so young." Tempest nodded. Her palms were sweating from nerves, being surrounded by people was not a good thing for her. She lived in a digital world of computers. People in such numbers were making her nervous and claustrophobic.

"Jason is on a quest to cure us all. You see Tempest, we are all sick with a virus that will destroy us. It is a contamination in the magic. The red eye tells us who is infected and who isn't. Most of us are infected. It also tells us the degree to which we are infected. Even Jason is infected though to a much lesser degree. He was chosen for the quest because of this. Magic is strengthening him so that he has a chance to help us." Tempest looked at Jason and Jessica continued, "that is why his eyes are solid green most of the time. Your eyes have changed too. You are not as you once were. In fact, I'd say they are going to be as green as his." Jessica chuckled as she watched Tempests eyes go wide. She waved her hand over a basin of water. The water changed to an image of Tempest. "The magic is seeping into you. Have a look."

Tempest looked into the basin and saw hints of deep green swirling in her blue eyes. Her eyes were changing colour. This is how Alice must have felt when she fell down the rabbit hole. It was time she started getting some answers. "OK, so what are these trials you spoke of to the cubs?" She watched as a group of teens organized the cubs into groups before running off into the woods with them.

Jessica sighed, "the trials are what created us hundreds of years ago. They are a test to prove we can handle the gifts we are given. You are human and will also have to pass them. They will give you some protection in our world, and limited access to magic once you complete the trails. There are six trials: fire, water, earth, electricity, air and lastly by faith. Each of those pups you saw will be partnered in a group for the first couple of years. They try until they pass. Usually, it takes until they are fifteen or sixteen. If they don't die they become a part of the larger clan, not just our small pack." She looked up to the sky, "tonight is the first, trial by earth. Jason will take you to where you will be running the trial." Without another word, she turned and walked away into the woods.

Tempest looked at Jason. She glared at him as he lead her into the woods. She stomped along to show her feelings. "Why didn't you tell me it was life or death?" Jason shook his head, "I didn't want to scare you. We need you. Now, come on."

CHAPTER 2

EARTH CHALLENGE

JASON LEAD HER TO A CLEARING close to the camp, no grass grew in the clearing. Contained within a square the size of a soccer field were boulders, sand and an intense heat creating a desert. "This is a Sand Snake Pit. All you have to do is make it across." Tempest's eyebrows raised in question. The kids were having a rope tied around their waists. "Do I get a rope?" She continued to glare at him, still frustrated that he had not shared more of what she was stepping into. Jason shook his head in the negative. "It's their first time so they have the rope. You don't have the luxury. It is your first time, but you only get one chance. You must succeed or die. You do not get a rope."

"You are going to have some explaining to do when I get to the other side." Was all Tempest could say. The pups were attempting to cross the sand. Few made it more than a few steps before turning back and running for the start or the sides. One try. That was all they had. One boy made it to the first boulder and climbed on top of it. The ten year old, the smallest and youngest of the group had gotten the farthest.

"If you get to the boulder you receive three minutes to rest, to figure out your next move." Jason explained. She noticed the sand churning around the boulder and the heat that was coming off the field. Her skin baking in the desert heat. Three minutes later the pup hadn't moved. The teenagers were getting ready to pull the rope when he took off like a bullet, running across the sand. Blinking to clear her eyes, the pup was done. He was being congratulated by the others that had passed the trial and by Jessica. Jason grinned, "one across, good for him." They walked to the starting line. "How did he move so fast?" Tempest had too many questions and not enough answers before starting a life and death struggle. She looked up at Jason but he had an insane look of pride on his face. He knew that kid, he looked like a smaller, younger version of Jason. "Werewolf" was all he said. "Now, kick of your shoes. You can't take those. Tie back your hair, it will help keep the heat off. Trust me."

Tempest kicked her shoes and socks off, tying her hair back. "How am I supposed to do that?" She watched the teens sprint across at lightening speeds. They they saw the snakes. Sand snakes. They were the size of large dogs. No legs, swimming through the sand. The snakes were a brownish gold in colour, matching the sand around them. One of the boys crossing suddenly placed a bad step. He screamed, he had stepped on a snake. His leg was gone. Blood splashed the sand and it came alive with snakes converging on him. Two large men ran onto the sand and another blew a high pitched whistle. A group of people at the far end started jumping on the sand. "They are trying to lure the snakes so they can save the pup." Jason glared at the group. "It used to be, you walked out into the desert and if you were attacked and unable to continue you died there. The slow and the weak don't serve the pack. Then the virus came. Now we have to try to save everyone. Don't worry, he will be tended to by the healers. By dawn he will have a new leg, as good as new." Jason turned to Tempest, "It's your turn now, good luck."

Most of the teens had made it across but they were far faster than Tempest knew she was on a good day. It hit her then that the snakes reacted to sound first, then sent. She walked to the start point, heat beating against her skin. She took a step onto the sand. She shuffled her feet to the first boulder. Climbing the rock she crouched. It was only slightly cooler on the boulder. So far so good, the snakes hadn't noticed her presence. Keeping her steps uneven to not give herself away, she kept going, unnoticed. She glanced back at Jason who was nodding, trying to get her to move on. Tempest moved to the next boulder as a snake passed within inches of her left foot. Her feet were bleeding from the rocks sharp edges. The sand seemed to pierce her skin. Her hands were just as badly sliced from the boulders as her feet. Change of plan. Tempest set off roaming across the sand making the next rock. She scrambled up, resisting the urge to check and see how bad her feet were. She could feel the sand mixing with her blood. "Just get across," she told herself. She glanced behind her and noted that she was halfway across. She noticed that the snakes were now circling the blood stained sand. They had her scent. She rested on the next boulder, only a few to go now. Looking to the next rock, it was sharper but only two meters away. She leapt, almost making it to the next rock.

She ran and climbed to the top. She tore her shirt and covered it in bits of blood and sand. Breaking off rock shards she wrapped the rocks in her shirt and threw them across the sand. She waiting for the snakes to bolt in that direction. The snakes turned and darted off. Tempest jumped and ran towards the finish line. She may not have the speed of the others but she had something she valued far more. She had intelligence. Tempest made it to the grass barely remaining conscious as she now realized she had lost more blood than she knew. She fell, Jason arms catching her fall, and lost consciousness.

CHAPTER 3

HEALING

WHEN TEMPEST WOKE, SHE WAS LYING on her stomach. Her hands and feet wrapped in bandages. Jason's mother was sitting in a chair. "What happened?" Tempest throat was parched and horse. She rolled over onto her back. "You sliced several important veins on the rocks. It caused you to pass out from blood loss. However, you did make it across. That was well done, an ingenious trick." Jessica really seemed impressed.

Tempest slowly sat up, her head swimming. She put her hand to her temple. "Wow, I must have lost a bit of blood." She muttered to herself as the room swam in and out of focus. "We would have healed you completely but then you wouldn't have been able to complete the trials. Since your human, though, we cleaned the wounds of infection and started the healing. We sped up you're healing to our own speed. But, this is only temporary. It will wear off in a few hours." Jessica explained watching Tempest.

"How long was I out?" Nodding her head, she looked for a clock and couldn't find one. "You slept twenty-two hours. You only have two hours to go until the next challenge. The next challenge is fire so I will say my good luck to you now and send in Jason with food. You should eat. You'll need all the strength you can muster." Jessica left the hut and motioned Jason to enter.

Jason came in carrying a tray of food. Smoked deer meat, flat bread and a bowl of vegetable soup. "Thanks for earlier, catching me and all." She was embarrassed she had passed out so quickly. "No problem," Jason said as he sat down beside her. He carefully put the wooden bowl in her hands to cradle. Her bandages made it impossible to use a spoon. She could drink the soup out of the bowl. He smiled and held a piece of bread for her. Tempest gave him a look that said. 'You have got to be kidding,' "thanks, but I'd rather eat under my own power." There was no way she was going to let someone feed her. She wasn't that helpless. She drank her soup, chewing the wild vegetables between bites. "So, what's the fire challenge like?"

"Fire is tough, really difficult." Jason tried to hide his grin but it didn't last. He burst out laughing. "All you have to do is get across a bridge."

Tempest nodded and smiled at his joke. "Let's get this out of the way. I want this over so I can go home. I don't want to be here. I want to go home." She finished eating, looking at her bandaged hands and feet. She hurt but she thought she could walk.

He nodded, "all right. But, I'll have to remove the bandages. You can't wear them in the challenge." Tempest nodded as he lifted one of her hands and started to unwind the cloth. The cloth was soaked with blood in every layer. When Jason removed the last layer she expected to see a bloody mess. Instead, she was confronted with white hairline scars covering her skin. He unwrapped the other hand. "How is this possible?" She asked, shaking her head. She ran her fingers over the scars on her palm. Clenching her fist, she stretched her skin but it remained unbroken.

Jason unwrapped her feet. "Well, since you are not a werewolf, it would have taken longer to heal. What my mum did was give you a bit of magic. This sped up you're healing." Tempest nodded slowly, staring at her hands before jumping off the bed. "So, let's go." Her feet were a bit more tender around the scars, but they were just as healed as her hands. He smiled at her, "if you were a werewolf those would be healed completely. There would be no scars. But, we could not heal you any further or you would have been disqualified. Not to mention it would have seriously messed with your DNA." Jason watched her amazement spread over her face.

Tempest nodded. "Okay, lead on. Let's do this!" Jason took her out to the clearing to her next challenge.

CHAPTER 4

FIRE CHALLENGE

THE CLEARING HAD BEEN TRANSFORMED INTO a molten lake. Sparks and flares flew over the wooden bridge, if it could be called that. Running straight across the middle was a rickety old wooden rope bridge. "So all I have to do is get to the other side?" She asked. Jason nodded. "What happened to the sand snakes? Where'd they go?"

"Magic. It all has to do with magic. Everything is transferred in by magic or transformed in some cases." She nodded as they walked. The teens were already lining up. All twelve to sixteen year olds, and there was the little ten year old who had gotten across the sand yesterday. Jason had a look of concern pass over his face then he shook his head smiling again.

"What's up?" She asked quietly thinking anything that worried him had to be a problem.

"Well, normally kids who pass the first one get intimidated by this challenge and back down. But he looks like he's going to try. It used to be tougher, but we can't bring a volcano here. Some things even magic can't do. We could travel to a volcano but finding an active volcano around here has proven to be difficult." She nodded, watching as the teens started crossing. Fireballs flew around them, over the bridge trying to hit the teens. Columns of fire flying at them, sparks and what looked like fireflies. It was the ten year olds turn fire flew at him just as he danced across running, spinning, ducking and dodging. He made it across with only a few minor burns.

It was then Tempest's turn to run, she walked towards the bridge. Tempest started across the molten lake. The heat of the fire burned her skin. The fireflies stung her skin. However, she was not going to let a bit of discomfort stop her. After the sand snakes, and the fear that had come with them, she could deal with a bit of fire. Lava shot over her, in an arch, dripping onto her skin. She let out a hiss as it hit her skin. She shook her head to try to clear it, this was much hotter then the desert. The flames shot towards her, she ducked, twisting around, trying to get past the flames as they made a wall of fire in front of her. She leaped up trying to get over the wall. Just as she was about to hit the wall, it dropped back into the lake.

Jason smiled as she made it to the grassy ground on the other side. "Good job! There's going to be a feast tonight. Everyone made it across." He smiled at her and they walked back to the camp with the rest of the people. Wonderful aromas were coming from a camp fire cook area. On the fire was a deer, skinned and cooking. All around vegetables were being chopped and preparing to be cooked. Children ran around playing tag or throwing balls. Jason smiled, "and this is what we are trying to save."

She nodded. "So there's a party tonight and then a challenge tomorrow. What is the next challenge anyway? Why aren't they deadly or harder? I get trying to make sure everyone gets through, but doesn't it undermine the virus, letting it prey on the weak."

Jason sighed. "That's just it. We need as many people alive as possible so we have the best possible chance at survival. Tomorrow the challenge is water which usually means a pool party afterwards. After the water challenge is air, electricity and then faith. If you are going to succeed on the quest, or even have a chance of surviving my world, you have to have the protection of the pack. If you don't then your chances of dying sky rocket. If you die, there is a good chance we all die." She watched him for any sign he was joking he didn't even blink.

Tempest nodded again. She wasn't afraid of death, she was however afraid for all the people here. If she didn't succeed they would pay the price. One of the kids brought over some food for them. They sat eating on a log next to the fire. As night grew closer they sat around the fire, listening to both scary stories and histories alike. The night was cold and subconsciously she moved closer to Jason. She slowly dropped off to sleep, leaning against him. When the dawn came she was still leaning against him though someone had draped a blanket over the pair of them.

She was woken by the smell of breakfast, oatmeal and wild berries with maple syrup. She shrugged the blanket off, draping it over Jason. Standing, she picked up the dishes from the night before. There was a tub of warm water waiting for dishes to wash. She went over to the pot on the camp fire and filled the dishes she had cleaned and walked back to Jason. Nudging him awake, "breakfast," was a muttered sounds as she looked at him sleepily. Jason straightened running a hand over his head, messing up his hair.

"Thanks." He said groggily, taking one of the spoons she held and mixed the oatmeal as though deep in thought. "You know you shouldn't play with your food. It will just get cold." She told him. He grimaced, shaking his head and starting to eat. "Ya not my favourite food ether. You know water and I have never really gotten along. I love to watch it but really I don't like to swim, it likes to try to drown me." She admitted as she ate knowing she would need the strength for the challenge. The burns from yesterday hadn't been dressed but they were still healing, the scars from the earth challenge were gone.

CHAPTER 5

WATER CHALLENGE

A S THEY FINISHED BREAKFAST, JASON GOT up looking at Tempest "you ready to go?" She nodded getting up. Together they walked towards the clearing. When they reached the clearing what Tempest saw before her astounded her. It appeared someone had picked up a section of river and placed it in the clearing. The water ran down the river piece to the end where it vanished without a trace. About halfway through, there was a waterfall that went against every law of nature. The water went straight up, then dropped from midair as though running over a hill. There were whirlpools and rapids to deal with. At the end however, there was a long calm stretch.

She looked at Jason "you're kidding me right? You cannot honestly expect me to be able to swim through that." She shook her head staring at the river piece which reminded her of the gorge river rapids. She shook her head again trying to wrap her mind around the falls. This water coming from the air was hard to comprehend. Jason looked at the teens already lining up. "Come on Tempest, you can do this, I know you can." He touched her shoulder. She looked at him. "It's just an obstacle course Tempest, and a bit of water." She turned staring at the course "just let the current take you and you should be fine." She shook her head in disbelief.

"How is that water even getting there?" Tempest watched the falls. "No wait, don't tell me. It's magic. You guys picked up a piece of a river and teleported it." She said sarcastically. He only nodded, looking at her. "I get it, magic great, humans not." She steeled herself before walking toward the line up, picking her place. She decided she would go first and drown then they could fish her out. "Sink or swim." She said to herself straightening her spine.

When everyone was ready to go, she jumped into the water. First, up the rapids. She swam like she had never swam before. Not only did her life rest on this, but the lives of all the people around her. She had to complete this quest. To do that, she had to beat these challenges. She had to prove she was strong enough to do what needed to be done.

Over and over she repeated how strong she was and had to be. She swam one arm over the other, kicking her legs, as the rapids pushed her first one way then the other. It got easier as she let the current direct her path. Before she realized her mistake, she saw the water starting to spin ahead of her. "Whirlpool!" She gasped as she fought the current. Putting everything she had into her strokes she tried to get out of the whirlpool. Suddenly, Tempest was sucked down. Spinning around and around, down, further underwater. She was far to dizzy to know which way was up. She struck out swimming, trying to figure out where she was under the water. Tempest swam into the hard bottom. Trying not to panic, she saw shapes swimming towards her in the water. She planted both her feet firmly on the bottom and pushed. Shooting straight up towards the surface.

Her lungs screamed for air but she was unwilling to open her mouth to inhale water. A voice in the back of her mind told her it would be easier to just let the water have her. She had heard it said drowning was like going to sleep. Her lungs felt like they were on fire, burning her from the inside out. Breaking the surface of the water, the air rushed into her lungs, cooling her lungs. The water splashed in front of her. She had made it to the falls. She was halfway through the water challenge. She swam on, letting the water pull her up, dropping her over the other side, headfirst. She hoped the water would soften as she hit the surface. She felt the water smash into her. She yelled as she hit. At best, bruises would cover her torso. She swam on pushing herself to go further. Ahead appeared to be calm water but she knew this stretch couldn't be easy, nothing in these challenges was. She swam cautiously forward. She felt something grab hold of her leg, pulling her straight under the surface. As she went under, it released its hold on her. She cursed herself for not letting someone else go first so she could see the hidden challenges. She resurfaced filling her lungs with air. She didn't panic as she was dragged under the water a second time. She looked around trying to spot the obstacle that had pulled her under water. 'A plant it must have simply snagged me.' She told herself. Then she saw it. Swimming back towards her was half fish half skeleton. The bottom half was fish tail the top half was a humanoid skeleton. It swam towards her, a bone trident clutched in it's hands. Empty eye sockets stared at her, it's sharp teeth mashed at her threateningly. She turned swimming as hard and fast as she could to get away from the creature. She looked at the fish swimming around her. They weren't right either. They were skeletons of fish. No flesh in sight, just skeletons. Within minutes she swam her way to the edge with these creatures following her. This was wrong. In nature, animals should not appear dead. She climbed on shore, feeling arms lift her out just as a bone hand raked her ankle, ripping her flesh as she was pulled from it's grasp.

Jessica, Jason's mother stood over her "Tempest…Tempest can you hear me. What happened down there. What did you see?" Jessica demanded desperately, as she set Tempest's feet on the ground. "Dead things swimming." She gasped, realizing Jessica wasn't shaking her. She was shaking badly enough that the world tilted.

"Dead things swimming?" She stated, looking towards the teenagers. "We are postponing this challenge. Anyone daft enough to try to swim it, will be stuck as a pup for the next five years!" She called over to the teens, "you can all continue with this challenge later. But something is wrong with the water!" Suddenly the water flew straight up like a bomb had gone off, then collapsed back down to it's original state. "EVERYONE AWAY NOW!" She yelled, before pulling Tempest away. People ran from the river challenge towards the camp. Everyone except for a group of people in black robes.

Jason stayed by her side until his mother gave him a look that warned him to get lost. She dragged Tempest into a hut, setting her on the camp bed. Jessica pulled on her injured ankle, to look at the scrap. She could barely feel her toes. "Ripped tendons and infection." Jessica muttered under her breath, "how could it be infected already?" Jessica looked at Tempest. "Skeletons right?" Tempest nodded slowly, looking traumatized and scared witless. She shook her head, "it's already turning septic. This shouldn't be possible." She muttered to herself, then to Tempest. Tempest looked down towards her ankle. Skin around the scratches had turned green and yellow, puss was flowing freely from her shin. The ground, which was grass even in these huts, was dying as the puss hit it. Tempest's hands started shaking as she watched Jessica. She peel away dead skin, leaving bone exposed. Jessica closed her eyes and took a deep breath. "This will hurt, Tempest. Just do me a favour. Hold still. If you pass out, fall backwards." Her hands started glowing a deep green. As her hands wrapped around the wound, pain shot through her leg. Tempest screamed. A howl of pain erupted from her throat. Blackness surrounded her as she passed out.

When she came around again her leg felt like it was on fire, though that was better than the inferno it had been. Jessica sat next to her on the bed. Tempest was drenched in sweat. "Don't move, don't get up. Just drink." Jessica held her head up pressing a cup to the girls lips. The mixture tasted of peppermint, sage, rose hips and a variety of other herbs she couldn't name.

Tempest spluttered. It was not the tastiest drink but it cleared her head. The room stopped spinning. "You've been infected with the same virus that the wolves have. This shouldn't be possible....your mortal. More than that, you are human, not a magic user. Unless, you have more magic in you then we thought…" Tempest shook her head slowly. "I healed your leg. The virus is still in your body. It will kill you, just as it will kill us." Tempest looked down at her leg. There were three long claw marks around her ankle. "Those won't heal. I'm sorry your stuck with them."

"What was that creature?" She asked quietly staring at her leg. She wondered what could do that damage and remembered the skeleton fish swimming without flesh. "The scars will be interesting to explain to my family if I ever get back." Jessica shook her head. "You will get home. Don't doubt that Tempest, have faith. The creature was a mermaid. There were fish as well, but something went wrong with the river. We don't know yet, the mages who summoned the river are being examined. There are also wolves traveling to the physical river. They are going to check on the original that we copied. Meanwhile, the teens who have to run this challenge are being taken to the river, where we get our water from. They will have to swim through magically made challenges, rather than the copy we brought in." Jessica shook her head as the girl slowly sat up.

Jason came in looking at Jessica "mum I'll talk to her for a bit, keep her awake and keep an eye on her." He said, in his hand he held a shovel and bucket. He dug the dead grass up putting it in the bucket. He put his hand over the bucket, in a puff of smoke the contents vanished "instant fire." He explained to Tempest before looking at his mom and nodding. "You go rest mum I can watch Tempest." He told her before sitting next to Tempest stuffing pillows behind her to help her sit up.

She poked his side "you said you would explain these challenges and everything else." Thinking now was a good time to try to get any answers she could.

CHAPTER 6

THE EXPLANATION

J ASON NODDED "YES, I DID SAY I would explain. What are your questions? Let me guess, the challenges?" She nodded, smiling. "OK the challenges. In the old days we would travel to each obstacle, hitting one every twenty-four hours. We would leave the wounded to find their way home or die. But as the humans expanded, we were pushed further and further back. We had to adapt and move our lands, our challenges, our heritage." She nodded watching him. "So you see, we kept our culture but lost our space. It's the way of the world. Everything changes. Then you have this virus, it hit us a couple years ago. At first we didn't understand it. Our people were becoming sick, we wound up getting sick. Then the weaker ones started dying. You'll notice, there are very few old people among us. They were the first to succumb. There are theories that humans polluting your world, now it's crossing over polluting ours. Despite our attempts to keep your poisons out of our land. It's only right that a human has to help us fix the mess. Your kind created it." She saw where he was coming from. The people who had made the mess should have to clean it up. "Do you want to go see how the challenge is going?" Tempest only nodded as she stood up. He took her arm and put it over his shoulder "just in case you need help. Not that you need it." He told her as she glared. She let him help her.

They walked out to the river where the camp collected it's water from. The well-used path was large enough that three people could walk comfortably across. When they reached the river, they saw that there were only a few people who were running the challenge. There was nowhere near as many as there were for the fire challenge. "Where are all the others?" Tempest asked, watching as the teenagers swam the water challenge. The pair sat beneath a tree watching events unfold in front of them. "People chickened out after one of the mages fished out a skeleton and they saw what they were up against. They will have another attempt next solstices or they have another hour or two left for this one." He glanced at the sun "two hours. They will stop it at four and bring forth the storms for the next challenge."

The kid from the first challenge had just finished swimming the challenge he was small for his age only four feet tall "who's that?" She asked watching as the kid was helped out of the water. Jason looked at the munchkin, then sighed, "that's Scott. He has two younger siblings and no parents. We wouldn't throw him out of the pack or anything. We would look after them. They are a part of the pack. But, he wants to provide for them. He wants his shot at becoming an adult."

She let out a sigh and asked, "they died of the virus didn't they?" The look in his eyes gave her the answer she needed. "Poor kid. We need to stop this virus." Conviction rang in her voice. "Scott wants to be an adult, to look after them. His little brother, Ethan, is six and his sister, Rachel, is four. I didn't expect him to get past the earth challenge, but now fire and water. He's doing quiet well. Air, though, that's the tough one. Electricity is painful but possible and faith, faith is difficult. It's also different for everyone, so we will see how the pair of you do. If there are two I'm hopping to pass it's you and Scott. He wants to be an adult, to take care of his family. It would also make him one of the youngest to complete the challenges."

Tempest couldn't help but ask "who was the youngest?" As Scott came over to Jason grinning from ear to ear. Jason smiled, pride showing through his green eyes. "That would be me." He picked Scott up, placing him on his shoulders. "You could be a kid for a few more years." Scott swatted him on the head playfully. He leapt into the trees above flying through the branches. Scott's hair was as black as Jason's and his features similar. "He's my cousin." Seeing Tempest's inquiring glance, he answered her look.

"I thought you guys were wolves not squirrels." She commented as she watched Scott run over the branches as though he was on solid ground. Jason let out a laugh. "With our agility is there any surface you think we can't travel over? Well, water….I've only known a few wolves who could run over water." He amended, she shook her head slowly and watched the river fall into a calm state. "A day at the river beach just what the doctor ordered." He told her as they got up, walking towards the river. A group of people wearing black robes stood around the river. "Those are the mages." Watching her studying them Jason commented. Once the challenge ended, they lost the robes faster then she could say gone. "No one likes wearing them. They cut off most of the senses, so they can concentrate completely." Jason realized she loved to ask questions.

They walked to the river side. Most of the people lay bathing in the sunlight or laying in the shallows. It was a wondrous place, with the sunlight shifting through the leaves, lily pads floated serenely on the surface. There were even fish, real fish they were not the monsters she had seen in the river. Scales of all colours from lime green to bright yellow shimmered. She sighed in relief seeing real living fish. People napped and wolves who emerged from the forest joined them. Resting along the river. "My kind love to run and sleep, we're up late into the night, so napping is necessary. There's the hunt once the last challenge is done. Everyone is gathering from around the camp. Even the ones who normally live on the fringes come home for this. The hunt is lead by one of the new wolves. The one who will be the lead of that group. They report to the clan council when things go wrong or when the vampires raid us. Anyway, it's a hunt for the new wolves. To prove they can bring back food to support the pack. It is a huge event for us all. Later this year, there is a clan meet on the way to Emor all the packs go back to the clan."

Suddenly, Scott dropped down in front of them looking at Jason. Trying to look as serious as he could, for a ten year old which was truly comical, his hands held still at his sides his gaze steady. "Jason can you start me on the last trial. If I don't make, it will you watch my siblings?" He tugged on Jason's arm to make sure he was listening. Jason nodded. "Scott, I'll say it again. You don't have to do this. We will look after you and them." You could tell they had had this conversation more then once. It was well rehearsed, each knew what the other would say. Scott nodded solemnly, "I know but I promised my siblings, my family, my parents."

"Yes, I will look after them Scotty, and I'll start you on the last challenge. No worries there." Jason ruffled Scott's hair gently, before shoving him in the river. Scott shot out of the water and dragged Jason in. Jason then turned and grabbed Tempest. A splash fight ensued between the three of them, soaking them in seconds. Tempest dunked Jason as Scott clambered on her shoulders. It felt nice to just be among friends relaxing, having fun.

When things calmed down, she looked at Jason, "why do I get the idea you're not telling me everything about this last trial?"

"Not here, later, I'll tell you later Tempest." He said softly to her, "only those who have run the last trial or are going to be running it this time may know. You must pass the others first. Forget about that challenge for now. You have to pass air tomorrow and electricity after that. It depends on when they can summon storms.

She nodded, "electricity what do I do?" They climbed out of the water. Sitting on the bank their feet dangling in the water. The forest seemed to lean in and listen to them. "You have to get through the storms. They are not ordinary storms. Mind you, there are vicious lightening demons." She nodded slowly hopping he'd tell her more. "There are fog monsters, wind harpies and of course hail hurlers. These creatures don't just swim through or float. They actively hunt for blood, like the sand snakes. They fly like the fire bugs. They will actively seek you out, testing your will, pushing you to your limits, hunting your electrical impulses. They will be trying to kill you."

She nodded "right don't get caught." She watched Scott and some other kids running off into the woods. They were running around the river, hunting each other, playing.

"Why did you give up being a kid to grow up? Scott I understand, but you?" Fish nipped at their toes. His eyes darted to the kids watching them. "I'm the alpha's son. My father is the oldest and strongest of the wolf clan council. I have to be the best for him and the honour of our pack. To run harder, hunt better and see more. I had to pass the first time. I had to run it, otherwise I would never be respected at the clan council." She nodded again hopping to hear more of his childhood. He smiled, taking the hint. "When I was a kid, my dad was always pushing me into things. There were sports and games between the packs, much like your world but with creatures and magic. There's a school that was started as peace mission after the war calmed down." He grinned, showing sharp teeth. They were sharp enough to tear a person apart. "I'd like to show you the school when this is over. It is in Emor."

Scott ran over to them. "Wanna come and play? The last one to the fishing poles has to bait them." He turned and run toward a man handing out poles. Jason laughed chasing him. He picked Scott up and made like he was tripping, falling, going to lose the race. Taking Scott with him, then he tossed Scott ahead. She ran to catch up to Jason. He let her win, saying he preferred to bait the hooks. They were joined by a crowd of little ankle biters all clambering for their attention. The pups pulled on their arms as they picked up their lines and helped out with the fishing poles. One kid was animatedly talking about a rabbit that had escaped her the other day. Jason shrugged as they climbed onto his shoulders using him as a human jungle gym. The water plants and fish were disturbed by the fishing lines as they dropped into the water. The fishing only lasted half an hour before the pups started getting bored. They pulled their lines out of the water. The pups dove in to catch the fish with their bare hands. Tempest pulled her line out, putting it against a tree with the others, before diving into the water.

She swam under the surface shooting like an arrow. The currents danced around her, aiding in her travel though the river. She found that she didn't mind the water as much as she had before. She swam to the bank and looked at Jason who was shaking his head at her, "what is the problem?" He chuckled, "the waters accepted you and Scott. I'll show you where you can find dry clothes when you get out." She smiled swimming back in the water. Tempest spent the next couple of hours trying to catch the fish barehanded like other people.

The sun set as a man ran over to Jason, who whistled to get everyones attention. "Time to get out of the water guys. They need more water for summoning the storms." A small group of black robed people formed around the river. The water level dropped and there was now a fog cloud floating in the air, five inches from the ground. Jason took her arm, leading her away and herding the kids ahead of them. "Remind me not to let you hunt when we finally leave here." He chuckled, she had failed to catch even a single fish. She had come close a few times.

"Can't we stay and watch?" Leaning and trying to see through the trees. "I'll get the hang of fishing and at least I had fun trying to catch them." Jason shrugged shaking his head. "Summoning storms is not easy. It's extremely dangerous. One distraction, one wrong move, and the magic won't be contained. It will escape and kill the people summoning it."

When they reached the camp, Jason took her to a storage building. "Most of us travel with a couple changes of clothes and do laundry in the rivers. Occasionally, clothes wear out or a kid grows or someone shifts accidentally.

So we have this." They walked into the hut. The room was lined with shelves, each shelf was numbered and on every shelf clothes sat folded. Pants were on the right, shirts were on the left. On the back wall were shoes and hats. Jason went to the back shelf picking up a hiking bag. "The numbers are the sizes. Now, pick out two pairs of pants and two shirts. Oh, and a set to wear." He added quickly. She grinned, picking out three pairs of pants. He left the building, going outside so she could change. In the corner sat a box of socks, in another under clothes. She found the sizes she needed, then tossed what he had suggested into the bag. A hat from another box she put on her head. She looked down at herself. Cotton T-shirt and a new pair of jeans. She noticed her own pack from home sitting next to the door. She went over transferring her stuff to a smaller pocket in the hiking bag. Shoes back on. Leaving the hut, Jason handed her a bowl of soup. They went over and sat by the fire. After they ate, he helped her find a place to sleep. One of the kids brought her over a sleeping bag. "Thanks." She said quietly to the kid before looking at Jason. "Thanks for looking after me." She lay down under the stars. She was tired of sleeping sitting up. Looking up to the stars watching them, there were far more here than there were anywhere else. She quickly fell into a deep sleep, exhausted from all the swimming earlier.

CHAPTER 7

AIR CHALLENGE

I T WAS THE THIRD DAY WITH the werewolves. Tempest decided
to start exploring the woods around the camp. She followed the children out into the woods, going along with them. She was introduced
to all sorts of creatures. From wood nymphs to a collection of satires, pixies
and fairies. Spending time observing the satires with the children, who were
teaching music, songs and panpipes to the group.

The kids and Tempest ate lunch with the satires. Talking of the challenges
to come, all taking turns guessing what was to come. The water challenge
had scared her yesterday with the skeletons. Tomorrow was electricity. She
was not looking forward to that. The theories on the air challenge sounded
like it might be fun. Everyone seemed to agree that electricity was one of
the most difficult. When she asked about the air challenge no one was able
to agree on what was coming. They talked of how it changed yearly. No one
really knew what they were up against. The satires talked of one year where
there was a cloud creature to fight. Another said the people were thrown off
a cliff. There was a rumour they were mountain climbing, though who knew
for sure? When Scott and Jason found her, Jason handed her a metal disk.
Scott held his in his hands already. "You're flying." He told Tempest as they
walked towards the clearing. There was a screech from ahead, in the centre
of the clearing stood a huge creature with the head and wings of an eagle
and the body of a lion. "Meet Greyhook he's a gryphon!" Jason informed her
smiling at her astonishment, the lion tail whipped around impatiently.

Tempest stared for a moment before following Jason towards the creature. It's feathers glistened in the sunlight. It's fur blended perfectly with the feathers. She shook her head, slowly, "that's amazing and impossible." They walked up slowly, Jason smiled. "A real live gryphon." She knew they were taking it slow for her. "I'm ok, really." She walked to the other teenagers. Greyhook turned around to her and Jason, staring at her as he lowered his head to look at her.

A pile of parachutes lay on the ground. The others were helping each other put them on, carefully checking the straps. Scott and Tempest helped each other, checking the straps and buckles. Jason came over and checked them both over. Nodding, he handed her the end of a rope. The end was tied to the gryphons saddle. "Don't let go," he instructed her. "Oh and relax this is a sport here, most of us enjoy it!"

The rope had a handle that she held onto tightly. One of the mages came around. "Step on the disk," he told her. She set the disk on the ground and he waved a hand over her feet. The metal moved around, her shoes holding her to the disk. The mage moved on to the other teens securing them as she had been. She noticed Jason was talking to Greyhook, before climbing onto his back. The mage followed him. After he had finished securing the teenagers, he climbed up behind Jason. Then they were off. Clearing the trees, racing up into the sky through the clouds at insane speeds. Most of the guys preformed aerial stunts swishing off the clouds. Scott looked less certain on the sky disk than the others. Tempest felt her feet fly out from under her as she flipped in the air hanging upside down. She accidentally righted herself grinning like a lunatic, laughing. She glanced at Scott sheepishly, who grinned giving her a thumbs up. She relaxed, letting the wind push her from side to side, trying to avoid flipping over again.

A gasp of amazement sprang from her mouth as they flew through the clouds. There were creatures emerging from the clouds. A world was up here, untouched by humans. No one she knew had seen what she was seeing. She would never be able to tell them what she saw. A nest composed of clouds had gryphon chicks roosting. There were other creatures completely composed of clouds. There were large cats pouncing wisps of clouds. These cats had huge angel like wings, made of white fluffy feathers. She looked ahead to Jason, watching as they were taken to land on the clouds. They came down on a soft cushiony cloud. Landing was a strange affair. The disks seemed to hover, waiting for the gryphon to come to a complete stop before dropping onto the cloud.

The mage who had come along moved among them, releasing their feet. She stepped off her disk onto the springy surface. Her feet sunk a little but didn't go through the clouds. She took a hesitant hop. Her feet sunk back to the same level, but no further. The sun shone high above them. From here she could see the earth far below. The sky curved around the planet. She shook her head, feeling adrenaline run through her. An insane surge to jump came over her. A voice in the back of her head daring her to jump, telling her she could fly. She took a step back from the edge, barely resisting the urge.

Jason was bouncing on a cloud petting the gryphons beak. He turned, looking at the group before him. "Well, here is the challenge. You have three hours to fly through the obstacle course and get to the top of the cloud mountain." He pointed to the mountain of clouds. Flying, soaring and diving around it were cloud creatures. At the top was a cloud shaped like a wolves head, thrown back as though howling. "That's the pick up point," he told them. Then he and the mage climbed on the gryphon. "GO!" He called, as they flew towards the pick up point.

She looked at the others who were splitting off in pairs or groups. Jumping and running over the clouds, racing. Tempest glanced at Scott, "I guess this ones a bit hard to replicate in the clearing?" Scott laughed, nodding. "Lets get a move on." They jogged through the clouds bouncing and jumping. It was like being on a trampoline. They flipped over the clouds, preforming tricks. They climbed over the clouds, the fluffy clouds speeding them along as they leaped over the higher cloud hills.

They were falling behind the others. Most of the werewolves were using the speed they were graced with to move across the field of clouds. She looked at Scott, "it's okay if you want to run ahead, I know I'm slowing you down."

He shook his head, "don't worry about it Tempest we've got plenty of time. When we reach the mountain we'll split up." They jumped onwards, finally landing at the base of the mountain. Straight up the mountain they traveled and saw large rainbows shooting out across the sky. Flying fish formed of clouds. Scott looked at her, "okay, your on your own. From this point on. Stay on the clouds and don't look down. See you at the top." He leaped away, vanishing into the clouds.

She shook her head as she climbed upwards through the swirling clouds. As she wandered upwards the clouds formed creatures around her. Huge cats, massive birds, dogs and even a few deep sea fish, swimming in and out of the clouds. She walked a little faster. She was trying to stay out of the way as they formed and reformed, the shapes shifted constantly. She stopped for a breath, getting increasingly nervous. She felt her palms soak with sweat, the stress and tension were getting to her. She realized this high up, she should be plummeting to her death. Standing on clouds was impossible. She knelt down, crouching, she felt on the verge of a panic attack. She heard her blood pound in her ears. She was light headed, her vision darkened as she started hyperventilating. "Calm down. Focus on your goal, now, what is it?" She asked herself laughing like a lunatic. "First sign of madness talking and answering yourself." She forced herself to stand still, her back to a cloud wall. "My name is Tempest. My job is to help these people and save magic." She started forward again. This became her mantra as she walked, forcing one foot in front of the other.

She ducked as she heard a shrill call from high above her. She glanced up. "Please be a nice normal small bird." Dreading the thought of it being anything bigger then a seagull. She took a deep breath to steady herself. The bird flew closer. Instead of staying relatively the same size, it was getting bigger. It was amazingly far away and proving to be extremely fast. As it flew closer, she saw it's huge pointed beak. The beak must have been as long as a broad sword but as thin as a fencing sword. It's wings beat hundreds of beats a second. The sound they made was that of a buzz saw. The colours were astonishing. Bright pinks, blues and greens, like a flying rainbow.

She realized it was a humming bird. A very large humming bird, the size of a pony. She was so in awe of it, she failed to notice it was diving straight at her. She ducked and rolled as the bird dove at her, missing by millimetres, with it's spear like beak. She hit the cloud deck. Soft and squishy, bouncing slightly to her feet. She ran towards a wall of clouds, expecting to climb. Her hands reaching out. Instead her hands went right through the clouds, followed by the rest of her. She was engulfed in darkness, hit by the freezing cold. She wrapped her arms around herself, tightly shivering.

She turned around poking her head through the clouds. Outside the humming bird hovered to the left of where she had vanished. She pulled back into the clouds. "OK options?" She asked herself "A-freeze to death,

B-get speared, C-run out of time or D...?" She felt around the clouds she had run through, she reached as high as she could. The breach she had come through was a lighter colour than the rest of the clouds, surrounding her were a stony grey clouds. She put her hand on the dark grey cloud. Her hand sunk in a little but nowhere near as deep. She found handholds within the cloud, on ether side of the breach, and slowly climbed up.

If this worked she would be able to fly to the top. If she missed, well, she would fall through the clouds and go splat or she would get speared by the humming bird. She counted to three and then launched herself out, landing heavily on the birds back. It lost a bit of altitude, then the ride of her life kicked in. The bird bucked, spun, dove and rose trying to shake her off. She gripped the neck feathers for all she was worth, holding on. The ride seemed to last forever, though she knew it was only minutes. The humming bird finally slowed, alighting on a fluffy patch of clouds. She hesitantly released her grip, stroking the soft feathers. The bird turned it's head looking at her. She smiled, "okay beauty I need a favour," softly speaking to the humming bird. "I don't want to hurt you but I need up in that cloud." Not breaking eye contact, trying to force trust and understanding across.

The humming bird blinked. Tempest took that to mean it wouldn't try to throw her again. She stroked the feathers on it's neck, releasing her tight grip. "OK let's go, I need to go up there to the top ok?" She gently dug in her heels. The humming bird took flight. It's wings beating faster than she could follow. They rose off the clouds, circling the mountain as they traveled upwards. Watching the clouds, she could see the werewolves fighting cloud creatures or bouncing around them. Here she was, getting a fast ride to the top. She laughed happily as they neared the wolf head cloud. She waved when she saw Jason and the gryphon. The humming bird hovered just above the lower jaw. "Now no spearing me when I get off." She told it and with that she jumped off landing inside the cloud wolves mouth.

Jason ran forward helping her stand up, as she brushed herself off. The landing had been soft and squishy. She hadn't plummeted through the clouds, as she had been fearing. For once, at the end of the challenge, she had no broken bones, no cuts and no massive bruises. Perhaps a bruise or two but nothing that needed healing. She knew it wouldn't last, but it was nice. "Congratulations Tempest. Not only did you pass the air challenge, you got up here first, well done." A huge grin plastered on his face. "That's the first time I've seen someone use a humming bird." Chuckling as the humming bird whizzed away from them. Jason put an arm around her shoulders, "you have quite a way with animals you know. You could come study at Emor when this is done. Become an animal speaker or even learn to fly." He tempted her as he lead her to the gryphon. "Greyhook meet Tempest, Tempest this is Greyhook. He is the lead gryphon at the flight school." The bird lion bowed it's head to her eye level, staring at her with one large eye. He let out a screech watching her. She winced, covering her ears. Jason chuckled, scratching the creature under his beak. "He's doing us a favour. When he's flying us back, watch for Emor, we will be flying over it to get back."

She shook her head in disbelief before going to the edge to sit and wait. Watching for the others. It wasn't long before others started arriving. When they had gathered, they flew down the same way they had come up. Just as Jason had said, they burst through the clouds and she saw the spiralling towers, glinting in the dying sunlight. Around one that looked like a tree, soared gryphons and dragons of every shape, colour and size. One tower was orbited by nine planets, suspended in midair. There was nothing holding them in place. They floated, rotating around. Another was thick with clouds part way up, but the top stood above the clouds. Everywhere she looked there was another wonder. It was gone in the blink of an eye as they soared away, back to the werewolf camp.

When they reached the camp, they landed heavily. Most people went off and found food or lazed about, already going to sleep. Jason and Tempest joined the cue of people waiting for supper, it was soup. Jason smiled, "every week or so we bring in game. Then for the rest of that week, we use the parts to make soup. That way everything is used. Waste not want not. You should get some rest. You have five or so hours, then it's time for the electricity challenge," Jason grinned at her. "It hasn't been twenty-four hours, and besides," she glanced at the sky "it's nearing dark. You can't be serious, it'll be night soon." He only nodded, "I'll wake you when it's time. Keeping the storms contained and up is a ton of work. We do this challenge when the fields ready." Jason picked up a soccer ball, going to play with the kids. She sat down and ate. She leaned against a tree, closing her eyes to sleep. She didn't feel like laying down, not tonight, when she would need to be awake again so soon.

CHAPTER 8

ELECTRIC CHALLENGE

JASON SHOOK HER AWAKE HALFWAY THROUGH the night. Getting up, she followed him towards the clearing. Just outside, they stopped. She saw that the group running this challenge was down from the original forty. They sat around outside the clearing, eating dried meat and drinking a ton of water. Scott handed her a bowl of broth from supper. "It comes back up with the least amount of fuss." One of the girls commented, "some prefer dried meat but I've tried this one before and trust me your better off with broth." She looked around at the people, the guys were dressed like Jason in cut off jeans, the girls wore tank tops and shorts.

Scott was dressed in T-shirt and jeans like Tempest. "They can change on command, unlike you and me. Your human and I'm to uncontrolled. It hard to change on command under stress." He explained, "yea, they actually shape change to wolves. It gives them an advantage in this challenge. The storm spirits don't see them as easily when they are in their wolf forms."

Jessica walked over to them. "Here's the deal. Anyone who wants to try has to do it now. If you don't want to, you can start back at the beginning next solstice. As you all know, this is not an easy challenge. In fact, the only one more dangerous is the challenge of faith. If anyone wants to back out now, we will understand." She said looking directly at Scott. He stood slowly, brushing the dirt off his shorts, "I'm first." His voice steeled and steady.

Jessica nodded. Everyone could see how determined he was by the look on his face. No one was about to challenge him. "Okay, take the lead Scott. As you all know, no spectators and no sticking around to watch. When this is over sit at the exit. Don't wander. Don't distract. We don't want any casualties, if we can help it."

Jason offered a small wave as Scott and Jessica lead them into the clearing. What they saw was solid fog. It must have gone ten feet in the air a perfect rectangle. Jessica walked to where they had entered the previous challenges. "Good luck." She told Scott, touching his shoulder and whistling. The fog parted, allowing Scott to enter. When he was through, the fog shifted, parting in another area to let someone else enter. It continued like this, every few minutes another person going in. No one had exited the other side. They were down to the last five, when it was her turn.

Tempest entered, putting one foot in front of the other. She found the fog formed solid walls, halls and tunnels. She realized quickly was why no one had emerged yet. This was a maze. The walls sparked with electricity, providing enough light to see by. A crack of thunder to her left, she dropped, rolling to the right. Lighting struck where she had been standing. Whipping her head around, watching for movement, she saw the fog shift beside her. She ran forward going down a tunnel straight to a dead end. The tunnel ended in a room. She turned to run back the way she had come and found her exit blocked by more fog. She turned back to the room ready to face whatever was coming. Fog swirled around her. The wind smashed into her, she fell against the wall. The fog was as hard as a brick wall. The wind was knocked out of her. The walls glowed slightly with electrical current, shocking her. She got up as the passage way opened, her limbs numb, her hands shaking.

Ahead of her, hail fell. She ran hard as fog swirled around her. Hail smashed into her shoulders. Fog snagged her around the ankles and down she went. She got up feeling her knees bleeding, her hands dripped with blood. Looking ahead, she saw an exit. Fog rolled over it. She ran forward, turning a corner searching for a way out. There had to be another way out of this, there was always another way. Lightning struck her hitting her right shoulder. She fell hitting the ground hard, twitching. Blood pounded through her ears making it impossible to hear. Her back felt like it was on fire. Forcing herself up she fell against the wall. Her balance was off. She stumbled, hitting a soft spot, she fell out into the predawn. Light! There was light hitting the leaves, leaves she was out those were trees. She stared at the sky, a light pink dawn was coming.

"Okay shut it down, Tempest's out!" Jessica's yell sounded far away. The fog collapsed and dissipated into thin air. Jason ran out of the woods. The others, who had run the challenge, sat on a bench. Jessica was at Tempest's side, "lightning burns, minor concussion, scrapes and bruises." Cataloging her injuries, Tempest couldn't hear her. "Jason since you couldn't listen to my directions, keep her conscious." She leaned down, resting a hand on Tempests shoulder and the other going to the side of her head. She felt her skin knitting together on her back. A wave of nausea struck her, her head was spinning. She could barely hear anything. Jessica snapped her fingers on ether side of her head. She winced, falling over. She heard nothing in her right ear, and only a bit in her left. Jessica sat her up, slowly placing her hands over Tempest's ears. A pain filled howl sprang from Tempest, her ears were fixed. The concussion was next to be dealt with. "Tempest you hear me all right?" Jessica asked Tempest. She nodded slowly. A finger moved in front of her face "follow." Jessica instructed, as she moved it slowly "Tempest, go join the others. You'll be okay." Jessica then turned on Jason. "What did I tell you?" Tempest got to her feet and walked unsteadily over to the others. She sat at the end of the bench. Jason stood being scolded by his mother.

Jessica walked over to them. "The next challenge will be at dawn tomorrow. You have the next twenty-four hours to prepare, and to hike to the tree. You leave at noon." She waved a hand and a table zoomed across the clearing laden with food from s'mores to roast turkey. A couple of guys started a small fire on the ground by the end of the bench. "Eat, pick your guides and move out." Instructions finished, Jessica headed off to check on the mages who had summoned the storms at the other end of the clearing.

They ate in silence. Scott had several burns on his hands and arms. Tempest watched the burned skin peel away from Scotts hands, slowly leaving behind clean skin. "Werewolf, we heal fast." He looked around before picking up a piece of paper from the table. "Write the name of your guide and pass it around." He wrote Jason. Several others wrote names. Tempest wrote Jason next to her own name as Scott had done.

Jessica came back, taking the list. "Rest and don't forget to say goodbye. You either come back as adults and full pack members, or not at all." She turned and left the clearing. Tempest let out a sigh as the others got up. One at a time they left for the camp as well. Jason brought her hiking bag to her. "Let's get a move on. Your human, the trip will take longer." Holding the bag, he helped her put it on. Jason gripped her upper arm and pulled her away from the others. Once they were out of earshot, he stopped and turned to look her in the eye. "This is our deadliest challenge if you fail, you die. There is no way to save you from this. If you pass you are one of us. It is a battle within yourself, a journey only you can take. The guide starts you off sitting in the first tree, focusing your concentration. The tree is where everyone has their faith challenge, since the start of the werewolves. Before the other challenges were created. Over eight thousand years, going all the way back to Atlantis. Anyway, those that pass are considered full pack members, with all the rights and responsibilities of the clan." He started walking and she followed him into the woods.

As they walked, she looked at him. "What does it feel like?" She blurted out, looking up at Jason. They past trees and plants of all sorts. Walking down the dirt pathways that were game trails. He simply looked at her confused "what does what feel like?" Absently, a deer walked across his path and he smiled. The spots bright white against it's brown coat.

She gulped, "the whole transforming into a werewolf thing. Does it hurt?" He shrugged walking onwards with her under the trees. Above their heads, raccoons and squirrels ran through the branches. "I suppose it did, at first. My bones shattering and remoulding. Muscles stretching and fur erupting through my skin." Shrugging, "yes it hurts. But in a different way. Some wolves go mad the first few times, but accepting it and not fighting makes an amazing difference."

She nodded walking on. Rabbits darted across their path. Hours went by in silence. It grew close to noon. They arrived at a huge tree. It must have been ten stories high. Eight people stood around. Behind them, a rustling was heard as Scott and nineteen others arrived. No one spoke, they just rolled out sleeping bags or mats. Within moments of their arrival, the teenagers had laid down to rest. Seven adults stood with Jason, talking in hushed tones. Jason looked over to her. "Get some sleep you'll need it." He took a sleeping bag and handed it to her. She found a shady spot under a nearby tree and was asleep in moments.

CHAPTER 9

FAITH CHALLENGE

D AWN CAME ALL TO SOON. SCOTT shaking her, "time to get up." She sat up and noticed the tree glowing. Jason stood next to the opening, a hand on the bark, smiling and at peace. The opening was seven feet high and two feet across. If formed an arch, the other adults stood around the tree waiting.

One of the teens held a bowl with fourteen pieces of paper, "draw a number." Going around until she came to Tempest. She reached, in pulling out a piece of paper. Eight written on hers, Scott had nine. They lined up according to their numbers. One of the guides turned from the tree, taking the first one in. It felt as though they had been waiting forever when the pair emerged. The guide went back to the tree, standing against it again. The girl, who had gone in, walked right past the line, as though they didn't exist. Her eyes were a deep yellow. No red or green. Her teeth were sharper, her nails lengthened. As she ran into the woods, she vanished. Her body changed shape, to that of a wolf. This went on for much of the day. Scott and Tempest grew nervous as two people did not emerge, their guides did.

Then it was Tempest's turn, walking towards Jason. He met her at the tree entrance. They walked in. Inside it was dark, but glowing green handprints lined the hollow inside of the tree, spiralling upwards. Jason sat down on the ground, motioning for her to sit across from him. "Why do you think you should be aloud to join us?" She stared at him as she sat. "Seriously?" she asked. He said nothing, staring blankly at her. "OK well, then I don't deserve to join. If I knew another way, to help this quest, to save these people

I would. I have no wish to be a werewolf. I only wish to help these people, this civilization, those kids!" He nodded sagely. "Put your right hand on your heart and your left on the tree."

She did as she was told. Placing her left hand on the bark, lights exploded in her head. When the lights faded, she was in a forest. All she saw were trees. She heard deep breathing, to her left a wolf walked forwards. "Lupa." She whispered falling to her knees in shock.

"Tempest." She growled, "you are not of my children, but you are here to help. We shall let you. But you need a gift, if you are to keep up. If you are to avoid becoming prey and to be protected." The wolf walked around Tempest, her brown coat shinning. She breathed on her face and Tempest felt stronger and faster. "Wake now child." Tempest opened her eyes. A scream tore from her throat as her blood felt on fire, leading straight to her heart. Fire traveled up her arm to her chest. She pulled her hand from the bark, the pain dying slowly. She looked down. Above her heart was a paw print, tattooed on her skin. Another on the inside of her left wrist, both sparkling green, pulsing with her heart.

She stood shakily. Looking around. On the bark, her hand print sparkled green at the end of the line. Jason nodded, getting up, he took her out. She looked at the few werewolves left in line and smiled. She was a part of them now and they a part of her. Then she felt it in the back of her mind. Their entire history, downloading into her mind. She knew all the werewolves came from the first wolves. The wolf mother Lupa and father Fang. She knew Romulus and Remus were among the first werewolves. She sat down heavily. This tree, it was the first tree, where their legends stated life came from. She shook her head, her mind feeling as though it would explode, blood pounded through her ears. Sitting back against a tree putting her head in her hands, it was to much to fast. As she realized, this the information sorted itself, falling back from the front of her mind.

Scott was walking into the tree. A few minutes later he came running back out, howling as the rest had. He now looked closer to seventeen then ten, taller, more muscular. The last few went in, taking their turns. When the last came out, Jason and the other pack members stepped back from the tree. The entrance closed quickly, sealing everyone out.

Jason walked over to her, taking a deep breath. "You were given a great gift tonight. You must have really impressed her with your answer." The guides started cleaning up the temporary camp site. "Where did the others go? What happened to Scott and the people who didn't come out?" She started helping to clean up. She felt better with something to do with her hands.

"The others, that's easy. They are testing their new strengths, the power rush, the smells, it is something you never forget." He smiled from ear to ear. "The people who didn't come out will feed the tree. They failed to give a good answer and would have made terrible wolves. Scott, he received what he needed to take care of his family." He told her as they heard a howl. The pack came running back, taking their human forms as they emerged from the woods.

There was something primal about them. The way they moved with an animal grace, no movement was wasted. They collected their bags looking at Jason and Scott who walked forwards. "Let's head back to the camp." Letting out a whistle, they started jogging back to camp. Tempest was keeping up with the jog easily now. Realizing, she too was stronger than before. She heard a howl from Scott as they neared the camp. She knew it was his howl and that it was the call to hunt. The wolves left their bags and their human forms behind as they reached the camp. Other people came to join the hunt, following the younger generation of werewolves.

Jessica and the children who had not completed the trials stayed at camp. She looked at Tempest, taking her wrist and examining the paw print. "Your bags will be packed while you and Jason rest."

Jason nodded, "thanks mum we will leave in a couple hours." He lead Tempest to a hut to sleep. She laid down on a camp bed and was asleep in seconds. These challenges certainly wore her down, causing her to sleep better then she ever had before. Her dreams were of wolves fighting wars. Ever changing battles. The dreams were jumbled, changing from peace to war from war to peace. It was the history of the wolves assimilating into her mind.

CHAPTER 10

ON THE ROAD

S HE WOKE THE NEXT MORNING TO find Jessica sitting, staring into the cook fire. "Tempest, what you and Jason are going to do is dangerous. The wolf mother gave you a great gift, don't squander it." Tempest nodded and sat down next to her. "In our history, there have only been a handful of humans chosen to be given our speed and strength. One still lives in Emor, others died or returned to their own time lines. Jason may look young, but if you count by your human years he's easily over four hundred. Young for our kind, old in your world. The vampires you are going to meet are far older, some are in their thousands. The ones who are going to help you are among the youngest, but don't allow appearance to fool you. They are still in the hundreds and they have long memories. They will remember the wars. We rarely keep track of our years. They become superfluous, after the first or second century.

Tempest nodded. "Is there anything else I need to know?" Watching her, trying to learn as much as she could, knowledge was power. "Don't bait them. They are quick to anger and slow to kill. They will want to lay a claim to you as we did. You are going to have to either let them or find a way to work with them, if you want to keep the peace. Don't let them see you shaken. If they do, they will think you weak and kill you. I'll wake Jason and you two can get a move on. If you don't complete this by the summer equinox most of us will still be alive. By the fall most will be dead. The virus is moving faster than Jason realizes."

Tempest nodded. "Collect the vampire and move on then what?" Jessica sighed heavily. "Then you travel to the first lake. Try to find out what's wrong with the source of magic and you fix it." She nodded and looked at Jessica. "That sounds too easy. Why not just take the pack there?" Tempest picked an apple from a tree nearby and took a bite. "We cannot find the lake, only a team of three can find it. A human, a vampire and a werewolf. In this case, you see, the lake moves. It is magic." Tempest looked at her, watching her eyes wondering why. "Because it is magic and there's something wrong with magic. Right now there are rules. Rules that must be followed, three is a magic number Tempest. I understand you have many questions but there are only so many answers I can give. Search your memories. The information is there." She walked away going into a hut.

Moments later Jason emerged from the hut pulling a T-shirt over his head. "Ready to go Tempest?" He asked. She nodded slowly, standing picking up his hiking bag and throwing it at him as she put her own on. "Goodbye mum I'll see you in a couple weeks." He tried to sound upbeat. They walked away from his camp, his family, his life. Now he was just like her. Stuck on a quest, unable to go home.

They walked for several days along deer trails and around lakes. Often, they were accompanied by deer and occasionally a couple of wolves. When they set up camp they had an owl roosting on a branch near them, keeping watch over them while they slept. Jason set up the tents, by enlarging small wooden figurines, using magic. The wooden tent went from being a few inches tall to a single person tent. Supper was a simple affair of soup and dried meat. After supper he started pointing out the constellations. Teaching her the star names and how to navigate using them. He gave her a stick with one end painted red. Before he lit the fire he would have her try using the fire stick. Tempest managed a few sparks, but not enough to light the fire. He seemed to find that amusing. Even so, he seemed happy with her progress. Every morning they rose at dawn, breakfast was dried meat and cold soup. They packed up camp and started off. They tended to just walk through lunch. As they walked they picked up wild vegetables to put in the soup for the following supper. During the night, before they went to sleep, they sat at the campfire. Jason taught her to meditate. He told her concentration was the key to magic. One morning when they broke camp he had Tempest try to shrink the tents back to their miniature wooden forms. He let her try for an hour. Jason tapped her shoulder, waving a hand over the tent, it shrunk for him. "It's okay Tempest you'll get it with time."

CHAPTER II

VAMPIRE PICK UP

ON THE THIRD DAY OF WALKING, they emerged in a meadow. There was no wild life, no bird songs, no bugs buzzing. In the centre of the meadow stood a large manor house. The grounds were filled with flowers. The house was five stories tall, every window covered by a curtain. "We wait here until nightfall." They sat at the edge of the woods. "Why don't we just knock?" From the look he shot her, she instantly regretted asking.

"These are not your fluffy emotional vampires with purity rings. These are cold hard killers. You've heard of Dracula? These are his children and they do not sparkle. Well, unless they are about to burst into flame in daylight." He spat staring at the house "keep that in mind." Jason continued, "the only reason they don't run wild killing and maiming is their blood donors and blood banks. The guard of Emor also help. They protect and police all the species, keeping everyone safe." He looked at the house. "The younger generation are a bit more tame. They can be just as wild if provoked. They may all look civilized in their suits and gentlemanly manners but they are cold killers."

Clouds passed slowly overhead. As the day wore on, she dozed in the sunlight, leaning against a tree. Jason, on the other hand, stood guard. He watched the manor house as though it were going to lean forward and gobble them up. Eventually, he woke her, handing her dried meat. "Whatever you do, do not show weakness or fear." When they finished eating, the sun had dipped below the horizon. A shadow moved to their right, circling to their left. When she looked back at the house, there was a man. He appeared to be in his mid-fifties, standing before them in an old Victorian style suit. He had brown hair cut short with bits of grey, but it was his eyes that stood out against his pale skin. Dark red like blood. Cold, pitiless eyes.

"What are you doing here Dog?" He ignored Tempest's presence completely for now. Jason answered, "we are here to request a vampiric presence, to assist us on a quest, to save the werewolf people and magic." Jason kept his tone even and respectful. There was a growling undertone of warning, daring the vampire to attack first. The vampire spat on the ground. "I didn't know you had such a sense of humour, Dog. Why would we save the werewolves? We have been trying to wipe out your kind for years."

Jason chuckled. "Yes, but if our kind dies, your kind dies. Our kinds are connected, if you believe the legends, the web." The vampire nodded. "We do, as you know. Now who is the tasty morsel?" The vampire turned towards Tempest. Tempest took a step forward. "My name is Tempest, sir. I am the representative of the human race, not a tasty morsel." She held out a hand to shake. He took it, pulling her close, kissing the back of her hand.

He took a deep breath. "Human with wolf gift, but also…magic. Come on. We will go inside. The Dog may come if he stays with you." The vampire turned to go back to the manor. "I am Eric, high leader, this is my coven." He lead them through the gardens to the front door. As night had fallen, the flowers of the carefully manicured garden had bloomed. Silver petals that smelled of blood. "The flowers are called BloodNights. We use it to make various poisons and paralytics."

They reached the manor house. She felt Jason tense beside her. "Stay close Tempest." Jason whispered. She was not about to wander off. They were lead through the front door into a grand entry hall. A huge chandelier hung from the ceiling. The walls, the room and the people were all styled from the mid fifteen hundreds up to the modern day. Those who favoured the modern were far fewer, favouring jeans and T-shirts. The modern and old clashed as her mind fought to comprehend the time gap.

She felt as though she had stepped into another time. It was as quiet in here as it was outside. It gave the room a dead feeling. She glanced at Jason he didn't look nervous just ready to attack. "Relax Jason," said a boy who looked around Jason's age. He draped an arm around his shoulders "we don't bite…" He winked at her his eyes as red as Eric's "…Dogs." Short spiked blond hair sat on his head. His features were sharp, hawklike like Eric's, he wore a black T-shirt and black jeans. "Now, now Vladamire don't scare the poor beast. I know it's been a while since you two have seen each other." Eric said, watching Jason for signs of attack. Jason simply smiled. "And bats are to scrawny to make a meal of."

He looked at Vladamire, ignoring Eric. "How are you bat breath?" Vladamire smiled, "I'm good Jason. Who is this morsel and are you willing to share?" Tempest glared at Vladamire and the rest of the room. Time to take a stand, she thought. "The next person to say what a tasty morsel I am, or to refer to me as food, will find out just how much fire I have." Vladamire at least had the decency to take a step back. "I apologies. I had forgotten how well wolves choose their companions. If I ever have the pleasure of dinning on your blood, I'm certain it would be better then our bland variety. Our humans lose their taste after a while. From the lack of fear." Vladamire announced. She realized he was complementing her. She also knew he was baiting her. "You smell sweet with fear though you're handling it well."

"Vladamire, I'm sure I'm full of vinegar. Now can we move on, we're wasting time." Tempest looked at Jason who nodded, telling her to go on. "We need a volunteer. Someone to go on a quest, to save magic and help save the werewolves." She watched the room before them. Most vampires paid them little to no attention, ignoring their presence. Eric smiled indulgently. "Perhaps if you would leave us to discuss the situation, Vladamire if you would." Vladamire clapped his hands. From somewhere in the house, came the sound of running footsteps.

The person who came through the door was human. She entered and went straight for Vladamire. "Sir, how may I help?" She was as pale as everyone else but she blinked and breathed, which was more then the vampires did. Vladamire nodded. "Please take our guests to my quarters. See that they receive whatever they might need." The pale girl nodded.

"Follow me." She turned and lead them down the tiled hallway. All the windows had thick red curtains pulled closed. Through the winding halls, until they reached a room. She pulled the doors open, ushering them inside. "If you need anything, just pull the cord." She motioned to a cord hanging next to the door. As she closed the door a click was heard as the door was locked from the other side. "Well, now what?" She asked Jason, "and what was that between you and Vladamire?"

Jason grinned, leading her into the living room. Looking around, Tempest saw couches and rugs. A wall of books and weapons of every sort hung beside them. They sat on a couch and Jason started explaining. "We traveled together, after the war. We were both part of the peace mission that helped build Emor. Before the city was built, we were a wilder people. War was still a popular pass time. We killed or were killed. That was before the last war. The first war, my fathers older sister fought in, she was a warlord. She's retired now. She teaches in Emor." He smiled as though that were a normal thing to do after being a warlord. "Ravin lost her children, she had ordered them onto the battle field. They were killed, all five of them. Their deaths caused her to fall from the battle front. She disappeared into the human world. When she returned, she brought a woman with her. She insisted we try to follow the humans example of peace. Not that your people have managed to keep peace. We have done what your species was incapable of doing."

"Emor was a small colony. Fairies and dwarves had found peace. An ability to live together. She asked them to help her build the city. The human helped as well. She was neutral, which made her a natural negotiator. She had nothing to gain, unlike the rest of us. A child from each of the three waring factions was chosen to 'help.' They were forced to live with their enemies. The lizards sent Rhydian, a dragon heir. The vampires sent Vladamire and I, her only eligible family member, was chosen, her brothers son. We traveled between the three factions, learning to live in peace. Proving that it was possible."

"We became rivals, Vladamire and I. We chased the same girls, played the same sports. We soon realized we couldn't beat each other. We always tied or the girl would simply walk away. We became friends and masters of mischief. It made getting away with trouble easy. Every summer we serve our time, as he puts it, with our kinds. Every winter we have fun in Emor. We are planning to build on the peace we have." He smiled. "As for being locked in…it's a safety precaution, for them. These are Vlad's quarters. I haven't been here in years, but it hasn't changed." His voice soft, as though remembering better times. "I came here many years ago, on the exchange program, to learn about each others cultures." He grinned and looked towards the door as it swung open.

Vladamire walked in, running a hand over his head, stressed. "Vlad, I'd like to introduce you to Tempest. She's safe to talk in front of. She is trustworthy. She won't repeat anything that is said. She's got all of wolf kind on her shoulders and magic. Do you remember the virus I was telling you about? That's what we are here to stop, hopefully." Tempest felt the weight of his words landing on her shoulders. As he spoke, the weight on his shoulders fell away as he told his friend what was wrong. "The council thinks it is affecting magic at the source. It's already started killing people."

"All right then Jason, let's talk. Tempest you may stay. If Jason says no secrets. Then I will trust his judgment of you." She nodded her thanks as Vlad sat on a couch, across from Jason and Tempest. Jason looked at Vlad "Do you think your father will grant us a vampire?"

Vlad shrugged. "He knows what we all know. Our species cannot survive without the other. I don't see how he can deny you. He may put it off as long as he can, to weaken your kind. The real problem is you Tempest." He looked at her. "The werewolves have given you the gift of speed, healing and I'm guessing the history of their kind." Jason nodded. On the table between them, sat an assortment of weapons and cleaning supplies. "I'd heard you were leading raids." Jason changed topics, "I was hoping it was a lie."

Vlad nodded. "At my fathers request, or order depending on how you look at it. I am the eldest. It is my job." He stared down at the weapons. Jason picked up a bottle and opened it. It looked like water but he instantly closed it. "Wolfsbane and nightshade." A hint of amusement in his voice. "Vlad, seriously, I thought we were going to bring peace." Vlad nodded. "We are. First I have to prove to my father that I can rule, so he will sleep...."

Jason only shook his head. "So what will they give Tempest?" He picked up one of the daggers, taking it from its sheath, testing the edge. "Pure silver. You are not messing around. This will actually kill my kind."

Vlad sighed. "Jason, that old trick won't work on me anymore. Dancing topics was part of my fathers training. Yes, I'm using real weapons. The wolves don't know I'm not there to kill them when we raid. That dagger was a gift from my father but you'll notice the wax coating one edge, so I don't kill." Vlad countered, "and as for my father, well, his main general wants to give Tempest to my brother, to be his blood donor."

"Not Orben. That guy is down right diabolical." Jason gasped. He looked at Tempest to explain. "Vlad has a twin brother, only a few minutes younger." He looked at Vlad. "Does he still torture the wolves he catches?" Vlad nodded. "Yes. Orben's as wild and cruel as ever. I get them out when I can and when I can't I give them a quick death."

She watched Vlad then asked "how does that count as a gift for me?" Vlad looked taken aback for a moment, as though it were obvious. "Well, it's an honour to be chosen by a prince. For a normal person, from your world, to be given to a prince is unheard of." Seeing that she didn't understand, he continued. "The blood donors for princes are chosen at birth. Raised away from the others, kept for the prince. Most donors feed many of my kind. The princes have one or two or even a dozen all for themselves."

Tempest's head whipped around to look at Jason. "You have got to be kidding me, that's slavery."

"It won't work. We need Tempest for the quest and I am not taking Orben." Tempest nodded quickly, agreeing with Jason who looked grave. Vlad looked at her and she suddenly felt very cold. "I could fight my brother for you and take you on the quest. The only problem I see with that, you would have to stay with me after the quest. Unless, I found a way to release you from that bond." He said standing and walking to his bookcase. He handed Jason a book. Tempest glanced at it. It was old leather with gold lettering glinted on the front.

"What is that?" Racking her brain for the strange letters and combinations "Finnish?"

Vlad flashed a smile. "Latin why don't you take a nap Tempest." She found herself nodding and laying down on the couch next to Jason. Arguments formed in her mind, but they floated away before she could voice them. Tempest had to rely on a vampire and a werewolf to get her out of the doom that loomed before her. Her feet rested against Jason's leg, her head on the arm of the couch. She was fast asleep as though she had been put under a spell.

She woke a few minutes later. She was fully rested and realized, with a start, that it was the next day. Jason had breakfast laid out before them on the table. Eggs, bacon, sausage and orange juice. She sat up, grinning. "Where'd all this come from? Did you find anything last night?" Vlad spoke from behind her. "The kitchens, if we want to be healthy our food has got to be healthy." She gulped knowing he meant humans. "Jason and I may have found a way to have you released. All you have to do is find a way to save my life." In his hand was a glass of red liquid which he drank from.

"How am I supposed to do that?" Tempest shook her head. "You are a vampire what could I save you from?" He looked at her as she sat up picking at breakfast.

Vlad sat on the other couch. "Well, we aren't impervious, just a little tough. Sunlight, rocks falling on us, even breaking our necks. Something as simple as falling over our own two feet off a cliff, can kill us. We are fast and strong. We do have amazing balance but it does happen." He admitted, looking at least a little sorry for her predicament. "It has to be me, personally, if it is I who holds your life."

"So all I have to do is find a way to save you but doesn't involves saving the wolves or vampires?" Finding the food good, she ate a bit more. She did feel as though she was in Hansel and Gretel being fattened up to feed the witch.

Vlad nodded his head, "you got it." He looked at Jason. "Remember it has to be my life you save. How about we go check on my father and find out what he has decided to do. I can at least push the subject."

Jason nodded. "Yea, let's go bother him. The sooner were on our way, the better." Jason turned to look at Tempest. "Don't interfere, their ways are theirs alone. Don't be afraid, it'll be fine. We will find a way to get you out of this." She got up, following him and Vlad.

As they headed down the halls, some of the doors were open. This allowed a view of the inside. Some of the vampires were feeding, others reading and some talking. Upon arrival in the main room, they saw Vlad's father and brother Orben, sitting on a pair of thrones talking. Orben's features were the same as his brothers, but his hair was black. When Eric saw Tempest, he clapped his hands. "Wonderful our guest of the night is here. This is my other son, Vlad's younger brother, Orben, Orben this is Tempest. Tempest for your gift you will be Orben's new blood donor." His voice held a sneer as he watched Jason, who was grimacing. Eric smiled satisfied.

Before Tempest could utter a word in her defence, Vlad stepped forward. "I am the oldest, she should be mine." She glared. She didn't want to be anyones. Jason gripped her wrist, warning her to keep silent. Orben moved from the throne to Vlad, standing literally nose to nose. "Why would you want her?"

Vlad smiled viciously, showing huge fangs. "Because father, it would anger our enemy." Glaring at Orben, "for me to take what he thought was his. Also father, I wish to be the one to go on this quest. I will need food. Can you think of a better supply?" He asked smugly. Orben turned to look at Eric, smiling menacingly. He pulled a dagger out and balanced it on the tip of his finger. He flipped it high in the air, catching it. Eric walked to Vlad, standing next to Orben. Vlad looked at his brother, "come on how about it? Don't you have enough to do here without going on some crazy quest with a dog and a human? I could use the exercise. Besides, you already have ten feeders. What do you need another one for?"

Orben watched his brother. Then he looked to Eric. "He is the oldest, it's his right to quest. But I believe I will fight for a right to quest. I could use an excursion." Cold, he was so cold.

Eric nodded, his red eyes resting on Tempest. "Very well, there will be a battle to quest. One hour before dawn, on the roof. Be there or forfeit." Orben glared at his brother before following Eric. Vlad motioned for the pair to leave. Jason nudged her arm, gently. They left with Vlad going up a stairwell, Vlad looked back at them. "I can hear your hearts. Do you mind slowing them down a bit? You're making me hungry."

"Vladamire, behave please." Jason said softly "Tempest is scared let her go." Around and around they went, going up a spiral stone staircase. When they reached the top of the stairs, Vlad opened a door. Through the door was the roof, on the roof was a stage. In front of the stage there was a single chair and a cage the size of a boxers ring. The whole roof was asphalt except for that space which had a metal floor.

Vlad looked at them. "If I lose, run. Jason I don't care about your quest. If Orben gets Tempest he will kill her and you will fail, so don't let him." He smiled removing his shirt. His skin was covered in white scars, as though he'd been in many fights.

Jason nodded. "I know Tempest is important to this." Eric and Orben came up with a group of other vampires. Eric went straight to the stage, next to the cage. The vampire boys walked into the cage. Jason and Tempest went to back out of the crowd. A pair of vampires gripped their arms, pulling them forward, to the cage side.

Eric stood. "Vlad, Orben. The rules are not to kill each other. You may maim, but not kill." He clapped his hands and sat down. Vlad and Orben walked, circling each other, before anyone could blink, they were moving. There was no way for Tempest to keep up. The blows that were falling were so fast. There was a splash of blood, a yell, the blows were like thunder claps as they hit each other. When the dust cleared, Vlad stood panting over his brother. Orben was laying on the ground glaring up at him. Vlad had a broken arm, but Orben's jaw was smashed, both his arms were broken. Orben also had a busted leg, bending sideways. Vlad straightened his arm, the bones crunched together, healing instantly. A white scar where bone had gone through the skin.

Eric looked at Vlad, "get your supplies and get a move on. When you return, we will discuss getting you your own coven territory or perhaps passing on this one to you. We will also be having a long discussion on your responsibilities to the coven." Eric stated before stepping off the stage and going back down the stairs.

Orben was helped out of the cage while Vlad lead them down the twisting staircase. When they reached the basement they were on a dirt floor.

CHAPTER 12

TRAVELING AND CLUES

T HE WINDOWS DOWN IN THE BASEMENT were the only ones she hadn't seen covered by drapes. It was predawn, the sky just tinted with pink. Vlad turned on a set of lights, with a switch on the wall. The room was set up to be a stable for all sorts of creatures. "Just let me grab my gear." Vlad said taking off up the staircase.

"Tempest, don't trust Vlad I know he's my friend but I wouldn't trust him if I were a human. He's dangerous and unpredictable. He is a vampire after all." Jason told her, "now pick a horse. We need to get a move on. I'll teach you about vampires as we travel."

They walked the room, finding an assortment of creatures. From gry-phons to pegasus, however, they chose horses for themselves. Tempest found a grey mare and Jason found a black with a stripe of grey on her head. They got all the saddles and tack together as Vlad came down. He was wearing black cloth from head to toe with goggles over his eyes. He gathered his own tack and handed Jason and her a pair of daggers each. "From my father. A gift and as close to a blessing as you're going to get. The sunsuit is mine." He got his gear on a brown horse. They headed for the door, leading the horses to the opening.

Ridding through the woods, Jason and Vlad seemed to be racing. They set a fast pace. Noon came. They stopped to give the horses a rest, and to eat lunch. That afternoon they alternated between ridding and walking. Jason and Vlad taught Tempest about horses as they traveled. When they stopped to camp for the night, they cleaned the hooves and brushed their coats. Tempest enjoyed the learning. She hadn't been around horses before and they were willing to teach her everything. Now that they had a vampire with them, however, all the animals avoided them. Tempest cornered Jason. "Why are the animals all avoiding us?" She set the fire, lighting it by pointing at the wood with the fire stick Jason had given her. "Light" she ordered. The wood it burst into flame. Jason grinned happily proud of her success. "Congratulations! Your first real fire!"

She smiled, "Guess I just had to stop thinking and let it happen!" She held the fire stick, proud of herself. She started shooting off sparks, until she saw his disapproving look. Tempest put the stick away still glowing with pride.

He looked towards Vlad, who nodded and headed off into the darkness. "Vampires are unnatural hunters. Most animals avoid vampires because they sense that." Jason told her shaking his head. "Lets cook supper for us. He'll be back later, after he hunts. He will need your blood, eventually. All vampires need human blood. Vampires can live off animal blood for a few weeks or so depending on the vampire. Then he will need your blood. He is an extremely resilient vampire, but he is still a vampire."

Tempest shook her head. "That is not happening. He is not getting my blood." Tempest fumed. "Why don't the horses run?" Trying to figure out how to avoid being a vampires snack. They went over to the stream nearby getting water for supper. The horses were wandering near the stream. They showed no nervousness at the fact that there was a vampire around, or that they had been ridden by a vampire. Jason smiled, "thats because they were conditioned for vampires by vampires."

Jason pulled a miniature of a cast iron pot from his bag, "enlarge" he said and the pot grew to full size. He then made soup over the fire, in a pot. When the soup was done, Vlad reappeared sitting across from them. He pulled his goggles off his head and pulled off the black hoody, revealing a t-shirt.

"Hey Jason, Tempest why don't the pair of you get sleep. I'll take first watch. Sun proof fabric." He said, seeing Tempest's inquiring look as she laid out her sleeping bag. She didn't bother getting in, just laid on top of it. It was to hot to sleep inside. She closed her eyes trying to fall asleep. Eventually, she did. It was an uneasy sleep, with every sound she woke.

It was an hour before dawn when she woke up. She headed for the stream washing her face. She heard something creak behind her, a shadow passed over head. She shook her head telling herself she was imagining it. She saw the shadow pass beside her. "OAF" she was tackled sideways. Someone shoved her to the ground, pinning her "get off!" She screamed as a hand descended onto her lips. Jason came darting out of the trees and hit the attacker in the jaw. She heard the crunch of bone, saw him fall as she ran back towards camp. She ran into camp and saw Vlad sleeping. She shook him awake, "Vlad wake up Jason's in trouble!"

Jason came dragging the black clad figure forward, throwing him on the ground. "Orben, what are you doing here?" Vlad sat staring at Orben, shock written across his face. Orben looked at them. "I'm taking what's mine. She's my human now. Give her back! Father gave her to me. The wild human will return with me now! You will not complete the quest. The wolves will die! The humans will be destroyed!" Jason shook his head. "The human is needed for the quest. Orben go home. We will bring her back when we are done with her, we will succeed."

"Now listen all of you my name is Tempest, I'm my own person!" Tempest realized this quest was all that she held dear. Her humanity, her spirit, who she was. "Jason, can we just get moving. If I survive this, I'll find out where I'm going. But first, I have to survive this quest with you fools." Tempest said loudly shaking her head.

"Go home Orben I'll bring her home to you, you can have her then." Vlad looked at him as he made sure his cloth suit was covering him completely. "I will be taking her home when this quest is done. She will be welcome among my people."

Orben nodded, "fine, I expect to see you there Tempest." With that, he turned and left, walking away. She couldn't help feeling pity for him. He was acting like a petulant child who hadn't figured out he was an adult yet. She also thought that was far to easy. She gathered her things, saddling her horse the guys followed. Soon they were ridding through the woods. They stopped to eat around noon just bread and vegetables then were off again. Where Orben was she didn't care as long as she got away. The whole time he had been there he had stared at Tempest as though she were a piece of meat, it had been unnerving.

Jason tried talking to her, but she refused, setting up camp in silence. Vlad took off, leaving an empty water container near the fire. Jason looked at her. "I'm sorry but you're going to have to give him blood eventually

Tempest" he informed her. "Don't worry about Orben we will find a way to keep you safe."

That night, while Tempest slept, she had a dream. The feeling of being pulled sunk into her stomach. She was running in the woods, hunting for the cure. She had lost the others in the mad dash wind blasted from behind. The wind pushed her onwards until she came to a sign post. The sign rotated, spinning like a top. It stopped, pointing off to the right. From there she flew like a bird, over a mountain, across a desert, over a waterfall, a rainbow spread beneath her. Stars twinkled over her head. She dove, crashing into a river. Following the river upstream until arriving at an ancient rock arch. There was a flash of light and a voice boomed "GO!"

Tempest woke with a start, kicking her way out of the sleeping bag. She woke Jason with her kicking. Vlad sat on watch, it was still dark. "Time to go." Tempest waited for them to get ready. They were on the move, the feeling still pulling dragging her onwards, it hadn't faded from her dream. "How does she know where where going?" Vlad looked worried "or are we just running from my brother?"

Jason shook his head. "No, we aren't just running. I think it's the magic, pulling her onwards or perhaps the directions came to her in a dream. It would be why a human is needed to find the source of magic." Tempest could feel their eyes boring into the back of her head. "A bit of both actually." She admitted softly "a dream showed me, but I can also feel a tugging in my gut. Now let's move!"

CHAPTER 13

THE CYCLOPS

LATE ONE NIGHT THEY WOKE, HEARING screams in the distance, echoing around the valley. "Stay out of sight!" Jason took off into the darkness. Vlad and Tempest sat quietly in the darkness, not daring to light a fire. They ate dried meat and some herbs as they waited. Jason came back around dawn. He looked worried. "No luck. It was too far away. The valley echoes weirdly. Thank you Vlad, for standing guard."

Two days later they found a village. The village had been burned to the ground. Smoke still rose lazily from the skeletal wood remains. They came across piles of skins. It was as though the bones had simply walked away without the skin, muscles or tendons. There were no bones anywhere that they could find. Jason nervously checked the ruins, looking for survivors. "This isn't right." He looked towards the sky. "The guards of Emor should have been here to stop this..." Jason walked towards the tree line whistling. A falcon flew out of the trees landing on a low branch near Jason. He stood talking to the bird for a few moments before coming back over to them. "We should get out of here. The guards will be here in a few hours, they can investigate and track whatever did this." He pushed the pair of them out of the village ruins.

"Did the bird give you any more information, like what did this?" She raised an eyebrow, not quiet believing that he could really talk to animals. He nodded, "yes, of course the falcon did. He is a falcon by the way not a bird. He told me that the skeletons just walked away. They walked towards the cyclops village nearby." The smell of burnt and rotting flesh followed them for several days. Tempest thought they'd never get out of the smell, then they came across the Cyclops village.

The cyclopes village was an interesting spectacle. The houses were single story, but they were huge, the size of the two story homes in her world. The cyclops were loud, blue and had large fang like teeth. The first cyclops who came from the village was particularly ugly. He lumbered up to Jason and asked. "Why shouldn't we eat you?" Tempest shivered at the greeting. What was it with everything in this world wanting to eat her? She stared at it's one eye.

Jason looked up at the creature staring into it's eye. "I'm part of the Guard of Emor, flyer division and you don't eat sentient beings." The cyclops nodded slowly. A neckless of animal skulls rattled around his neck. Tempest looked up he had skull earrings, little hair and wore a belted loincloth. The houses were wood and mud huts. She came up to the cyclops's knee. Jason came up to the waist, these creatures were giants. The cyclops smiled, "very smart guard but what qualifies at sentient that is the true question. What news do you bring from Emor?"

Jason smiled at ease here. "No news. I'm on summer leave and on a quest. I am Jason, this is Vlad and Tempest." He introduced them to the cyclops who's eye landed on each of them as they were introduced. "I am Dave, welcome to our home. Jason if you do not mind could you send word to the flyers. We require their presence, we have a slight problem." The cyclops smiled down at them. Jason nodded, "what is your problem. Perhaps I can help?" Dave waved his hand to dismiss the idea. "In the morning Jason, tonight we feast with you. You are our guests." He lead them to the central fire where the feast was to take place.

The cyclops were decent cooks, using many different spices. Roast pigs the size of cows turned on spits over fires all around. The three of them sat with Dave, eating and chatting about the area and travel. After supper they were shown to a wood and mud hut. The inside was cosy and warm, despite the fact that it was made with mud. There were four bunk beds and a small table with chairs, normal size. This hut was made for guests. Dave came in making the furniture look tiny compared to him. "This is where the guards stay when they are with us. You are welcome here. I will come get you in the morning. Sleep in peace, you are safe here." And with that, he left. Tempest climbed the ladder to the top bunk, putting her arms behind her head. "This place is crazy guys." She closed her eyes, letting out a sigh. "Are we really safe here?" She asked starting to doze off.

"Yes, here is safe. I've stayed here several times before. The cyclops are good people. The only place safer, is the city of Emor." Vlad said smiling. He looked over at Jason, "think they still play chess?" Jason chuckled, "oh probably. Are you going to go play?" Tempest heard Vlad, "of course. See you later Jason." She heard the door slam shut behind him.

Jason woke her in the morning, shaking her arm, "time to wake." Vlad was already awake. He stood talking with Dave.

Dave took them out to the edge of the village, where a holding pen they had built. Inside the holding pen was a rattling like bones shifting. As they got closer, they saw the shape was that of a cyclops, but it was mostly bones. The flesh was falling off. "Great zombies, I love zombies", Tempest said sarcastically. She nervously ran a hand through her hair.

Dave shook his head, "it took five of us to capture it. Two have gone crazy and are in other pens nearby. A third was killed as we captured the skeleton." They walked to the pens holding the two who had gone crazy. As they approached, the creatures inside lurched at the wooden slats, trying to attack. As the pen shook, Tempest took a jump backwards. Dave looked at them. "I've never seen an infection like it. I studied in Emor I've got a medical degree. This is wrong."

Soon after they saw the skeletons, they left the village. They followed Tempest's gut feeling once more. Each night Jason had her set up camp. He told her the same thing before she went to sleep every night. "Knowledge can save a life and knowing your abilities is apart of knowing yourself."

CHAPTER 14

✳

CENTAURS AND SIGNS

A FEW DAYS AFTER THEY HAD LEFT the cyclops village, they ran into a group of centaurs. The centaurs were hunting dead creatures, the skeletons. Tempest walked forward, holding her hands in front of her, showing they were empty. "Hello, I am Tempest. These are my quest mates: Jason and Vladamire. We seek information. Do you know of a sign post in the woods. It would be tall and rotate?"

A roan centaur walked forward. "I'm Aidan. Yes, I know of the sign post. Will you submit, so we know you are not infected?" It was then she noticed the bows were drawn, ready to shoot. Tempest shrugged, "we can hold intelligent conversations and our skin isn't falling off." One of the centaurs came forward, holding a torch. He waved it in front of them, then moved behind them. No one moved. Aidan seemed satisfied, "we've found the creatures are afraid of fire. If you wish we can escort you to the sign post."

They traveled with the centaurs for several days. While traveling, Vlad and Jason broached the subject of who Tempest belonged to. She shut down and refused to speak to either of them. When they finally reached the sign post, she was astonished to find it was taller then most trees. What was far more amazing, however, was the fact that all the signs rotated to point in one direction. The direction they needed to travel. "It works on magic. It tells you which way you must travel." Aidan said to them before he and the centaurs took off riding away. "If you have no need for direction, it tells you where everything is."

Tempest stared up at the sign post Emor, Werewolf camp, Human world, Hawk Ridge, Dark forest, Rain Forest, Desolate Desert, Snow Mountain... there were to many names to read and to many places. However, at present they all pointed in the same direction. They traveled east, east towards the sunrise. Vlad continued to travel wrapped in his sunsuit and hunting at night. Jason and Tempest searched for food by daylight, they gathered herbs and berries. They had already been traveling for a month. Tempest was growing tired of Vlad, and his watching her every move. The hunger in his eyes after his hunt every night.

One night while they were traveling, Jason sat Tempest down. "He's going to need to feed soon Tempest." She only nodded she knew that he needed blood, human blood to survive.

CHAPTER 15

SNOW MOUNTAIN

A S THE DAYS PASSED, THE TREES became shorter, more shrub like. The terrain become more rocky. Eventually, they were traveling up a mountain. When the horses started to lose their footing they were released. "They will find their way home. They are trained to return to the vampire manor." Vlad explained, looking at them when they camped one night. He attached everything they didn't need to the saddles. Taking only what they could carry, before he released the horses. They took off, back the way they had come, to the vampire manor.

As they climbed the mountain, it became colder and harder to breath. The air was growing thinner the higher they traveled. Jason took to sleeping in his wolf form next to Tempest, to help keep her warm. They were just reaching the top when Tempest walked into a yeti.

Yetis are like ogres. Except for a few differences. They are covered in fur and have much bigger feet. Their foreheads come down over their eyes, to protect them from snow blindness. The yeti hugged Jason. "Welcome to my mountainside, wolf!" She said putting him back on the ground "I received word from Emor that you may be coming up my way. All outposts have been put on watch for you. I am glad you found mine." She glared at Vlad, then ignored him. She took them back to her cave. It was a small entrance. The yeti fit, seeming to be able to collapse her bones. She was more fur then she appeared.

It was a cozy cave. It wasn't damp or even dark, once she lit the oil lamps. There was a bed sitting against one wall, a table and many books, sitting on shelves and the tables. "Yetis are solitary creatures. We only occasionally gather. Usually at a solstice. The new year and holidays." She explained, "you are welcome to spend the night here with me. But, the vampire sleeps outside." Vlad nodded, unaffected by the cold, he set up camp outside. "I am Sara it is nice to meet you both."

Jason and Tempest spent the night with the yeti, camped out on the floor. Sara spent the night telling stories of her people. Of the meetings with her people. Ancient tales of when the yeti people roamed the world. How the humans first began encroaching on wolf territory, which pushed the yetis up further north. Tempest fell asleep, listening to her talk of the old days with Jason.

Sara was gone by dawn when Jason woke her, gently saying, "it's time to go." Vlad met them at the doorway and they started traveling. Sara had refilled their food supplies while they slept. Leaving them snow shoes and extra blankets for the rest of the trip.

When they reached the top of the mountain, far far below them they saw a vast desert laid out. Tempest looked at Jason, then Vlad. "We have to cross that." She stared down before they slowly descended. The desert slowly came up to meet them. When it went from snowing to raining, they removed their snow shoes, leaving them in the last cave down. The temperature went from freezing to baking hot. The desert heat rising to meet them, by the time they were halfway down. The side of the mountain trees had started growing again. Short, then slowly growing in hight. As the land grew hotter, the trees became shorter. The ground became harder, the terrain was rougher. When they did reach the last of the trees, near the bottom, they made camp.

CHAPTER 16

DESOLATE DESERT

I N THE MORNING, THEY FINISHED THE trek down the mountain. When they started into the desert, Jason looked at Tempest. "This is one of the homes of the sand snakes. We must be carful. There is, or was a clan of dingos here the last time I was through." Jason sighed, shaking his head. "We were run out of here by the barking lunatics, they are a wild people. The laws of Emor stop here. This is a place of banishment."

Vlad glared over the desert, tilting his head. "The temperature, for the next few days, is hotter then hell." He imitated a weather man. "Are you sure we have to go this way Tempest?" She only nodded. Tempest only talked to Vlad when she had to. It was decided they would cross the desert by night, when it was cooler. They would sleep during the day.

The first night in the desert, when they stopped for the day, Jason nicked her arm, filling the canteen for Vlad with her blood. He had said nothing and they didn't mention it. Vlad started leaving whatever food he found next to the tent entrance. It was usually herbs and sometimes a small animal, food was scarce in the desert.

They traveled across the desert as night fell, counting on her sense of direction to guide them. They shuffled across the sand, keeping their steps uneven and without pattern. They heard howling in the distance. It was impossible to tell how far away it was. Sound travelled differently in the desert than it did in for the forest. Vlad wore a hoody and dress pants. He looked, for all the world, like a university student, despite the fact that they were in a desert. During the day he wore his sunsuit. At night he relaxed, wearing only his T-shirt and dress pants.

Ahead of them a huge shape emerged from the sand illuminated by moonlight, the creature had legs and was running across the sands toward them. It slowed slightly, though not nearly enough as it overshot them. It spun around to give chase as they ran. Knowing even as they ran, they had no chance of escape.

Jason took his werewolf form and she saw his full size in action for the first time. She saw what a monster he was standing on his hind legs. He was covered in fur. His head was that of a wolf, his arms were human shaped covered in fur. Thick muscles cording around his bones. He threw his head back, howling loudly. The sound chilled her to the bone. He stood ready, turning to fight. Vlad followed Jason's lead, turning to fight, as did Tempest. They were not going let Jason face this creature alone!

Vlad had three inch fangs sticking out of his mouth. His nails had become claws. His eyes blazed a dark red. He rolled up his sleeves while they waited for the lizard to come back around, "well this should be fun." He then looked at Tempest, who had the pair of daggers Vlad had armed her with. Jason simply chuckled and tapped Vlad on the shoulder.

The giant lizard circled back around to them, rearing up on it's hind legs in front of them. When his front claws hit the ground, it shook beneath them, causing Tempest to stumble. Way up, on the back of the lizards neck, there was a woman on top of the lizard. She called down to them, "surrender and you won't be eaten!"

Jason growled loudly, "we are on a quest to save magic leave us!" Vlad took a step forward, glaring. "Remove yourself from our path in the name of Vladamire of the clan Dracula, prince of darkness, next in line for king." Tempest glared, yelling, "move unless you plan to help!"

The lizard lashed it's tongue out wrapping it around Tempest. She screamed as she was covered in slime. Screaming her head, off she was sucked off the ground and carried into the creatures mouth. It was dark slimy and stunk of rotten meat. Worst of all, there was no sound. She reached for her daggers, to stab it's tongue. Scaring the lizard into dropping her or to slice the tongue off, only to find she'd dropped her daggers. She didn't move, afraid the lizard would swallow her. Before she could think of what to do next, besides not panic, she was spat out into the sand, surrounded by people covered in shed lizard skins, scales and warpaint. Their eyes were like a snakes, slits against the torches they held. The group must have numbered close to thirty. Surrounding them. Jason and Vlad stood above her. Jason helped her to her feet. He had already returned to his human form, his clothes in scraps. "You will come with us. You are charged with trespassing in the Land of Scales. You will be put on trial. Then sentenced to imprisonment: work in the fields or death." The woman said. She had been on the lizards back. Looking closely, Tempest realized it was a huge bearded dragon.

One of the men walked forward, binding their hands in front of them with a silvery vine. Jason let out a hiss as it touched his skin, as did Vlad. Tempest felt nothing. Jason growled as they hoisted her, shoving her in a wagon. The wagon was attached to a smaller lizard. The wagon had bars on three sides and a back ramp that was slammed shut. There were a pair of guards who came in with them. Standing on guard in the back of the wagon. For growling one guard hit Jason over the head. It was then she noticed their lizard tails, and the neck frill on one of the guards. They didn't just wear skins, they were lizards. Their skin was reptilian. "They are called Reptos. Vampires and werewolves are both weakened by these bonds. The silver is for Jason and for me it's part of the plant they harvest this crap from." Vlad said agitated.

"Silence!" The guard with the frill growled. One of the guards spat over them and Tempest felt her skin start tingling. Then, she blacked out.

CHAPTER 17

LAND OF SCALES

WHEN TEMPEST WOKE, SHE WAS ALONE, in a cell underground. Getting up slowly, taking in her surroundings. Water dripped from the ceiling in one corner. A bed, made of stone, was carved into the wall. A hole in the floor, where the water moved sluggishly, served as the toilet. The cell was five by five. She looked beyond the bars of her cell. Jason and Vlad were across the hall in their own cells. She had the luxury of movement, they were tied to the back wall. A chain attached to collars and wrist cuffs. The chain allowed them to move, but they could not reach the bars. Tempest watched them, looking up and down the hall going to the bars of her cell. "Where are we guys?" She shivered against the cold, it was freezing.

Vlad was the first to answer. "We were captured by reptos. We are above one of their cities. In a jail. The cold makes people more compliant." He and looked toward Jason's cell. "Hey brother, you okay?" Jason groaned, his hand going to his head. "So not good! Repto's love devouring warm bloods, as they call us. They also like working us where their kind can't. Their normal prey is dingos. The thin air, cold and yetis of the mountain keep them confined to the deserts. Oh and they are cannibalistic." At this point Tempest was shaking, more than just the cold bothered her. "Did I leave anything out Vlad?"

Vlad shook his head, "only that their cities are hot. Other then that, I think that's about everything. Tempest look, don't provoke them." She was tired of being told to be careful.

One of the guards, a humanoid bearded dragon, came down. He set the bars ringing as he went, with his wickedly curled claws. He stopped outside Jason's cell, looking at him. "You'll be going down to the mines with the bat. Your human is to work entertaining us in other ways, as prey and serving as a servant." He hissed, his tongue darting out of his mouth as he licked his claws.

Jason launched himself at the bars, coming up short, pulled back by the chain. "Over my dead body, you cold blooded monster." The lizard laughed, "that can be arranged dog. Though I think I'll prefer to have you watch, as we peel her skin off. Slice by slice." The Repto guard opened her cell. More guards came down the hall, opening Vlad and Jason's cells. They descended like a storm, attacking the men, beating them senseless.

The repto who came into her cell, pulled her out and down the hallway. He lead her through a maze of passage ways to a room. This room was filled with girls, all washing dishes and doing laundry. They were of every species. All had collars, like the guys. All tied to the walls. The repto guard grinned, "when the trial ends, this is where you'll wind up. Your friends will wind up dead, in the mines." He took Tempest back to her cell.

"So I have dirty dishes and laundry to look forward to?" Tempest asked sarcastically, a blow fell on the top of the head and she was thrown back into her cell. The cell door slammed shut behind her. The key clicking into place. When the repto guard left, her she looked over at her friends. "You okay guys?"

Vlad groaned, getting up. "Yea don't worry, just a little intimidation. We vampires used to use that tactic." He shook his head in disgust. "My brother still does."

Jason slowly rose, "I'm all right too. I'm stronger then I look." He stood only to sway slightly and lean against the wall. Vlad chuckled as Jason glared at the wall separating them. "How do you always know?" Jason shook his head. "Every time we get captured or sent to jail, you know."

He burst out laughing. "Because Jason, the wall, which I'm sure you're leaning against by now, has stood fine on it's own for years." Jason sighed leaning against the wall and sliding down it to sit. "Good Jason, you need to relax. We have run into worse situations than this."

"Point made! Now" Jason said clapping his hands together, "plans who's got them?"

"I've never known anyone to escape the Reptilians." Vlad admitted, looking sheepish.

Tempest stood walking to her cell door. She wrapped her hands around the bars. "OK, the plan A-get out of these cells. B-rescue the girls held captive and stuck doing chores. C-snag one of those giant lizards and ride to safety." She ticked them off her fingers as she went. "First problem, the cell doors. Where are the keys? I believe they are on the heard guard. Ergo, I must steal them, because there is no way he will let you guys near him. He, like you guys, underestimates me." She shook her head. "Where are their weak spots?" She asked sitting back on her heels, balancing.

Vlad shook his head. "I've got nothing Tempest. My people avoid the desert. The heat and light usually prevent my people from being out here. Sunsuits are a relatively new invention. My people, even with them, we don't like the heat. What about you Jason?"

Jason just shook his head, sighing, "they are the ultimate predator. They can even regrow lost limbs. Get some rest Tempest. We will think of something." He said softly. Tempest nodded and laid on the rock block that served as her bed. She rested, knowing she had to be ready, if what she was planning was to work.

CHAPTER 18

ESCAPE

SHE HEARD A WHISTLE AND WOKE. She sat up and looked across to Vlad. He stood at his bars, "guards coming." His voice barely above a whisper.

"Okay. Keep Jason out of this. I'll handle the guard and get the key." She hissed as Vlad nodded. The guard came down the hall, rattling the bars as he approached her cell. He opened it slowly. Tempest would have glared, but the idea was to steal the keys. Not to be beaten, as the guards had beaten Jason and Vlad. He looked at her when she walked to the cell door. To the guard she asked, "Sir perhaps you could take me out of this cell for a walk."

He grinned, "I knew you'd be the first to break." He opened her cell door and lead her down the hall, away from the others. Her back hit the wall. She was shoved against it, the Repto guard held her there. Tempest let her hand go to his belt, hunting for the key ring. Her other hand went to the back of his neck. She pulled the key loop before she gripped the back of his neck. He struggled against her. She brought her other arm across his throat, cutting off his oxygen. He passed out and she left him fall to the floor.

Despite his threats, she was not a killer, nor did she wish to become one. Tempest ran back to the cells, unlocking Jason's cell first. She went to his collar trying to unlock it. Jason shook his head "wall, go to the wall!" He told her. She went to it, unlocking the chain from the wall. Then she went to Vlad's cell. Unlocking his door and his wall chains. Jason stood at Vlad's door. His chain curled in his hand, "come on, let's go." Jason watched as

Vlad gathered his chain as well. "The collars have unique locks, the walls are all the same."

Tempest lead them down the halls, back towards the chore room. She split the keys between the three of them. When they reached the door, she looked at Jason and Vlad. "We get these girls out, then find a lizard to ride and get out!" Jason and Vlad nodded. They went into the chore room, each starting in a different area of the room. When one key bunch failed they moved on, letting one of the others try. They had everyone released in a little over five minutes. Over fifty girls stood staring at Tempest and her friends.

Tempest looked to Jason, "listen up girls. Does anyone know a way to the stables? The plan is to ride our way out." He called to them. Tempest was happy to let him take charge. Vlad stood at the door, keeping watch for them. One of the youngest, only twelve walked forward. She was short, four foot five. Short brown hair, dark skin. Her eyes a deep gold colour, like the sands they had travelled over. Her ears twitched on the top of her head. She was one of the dingo creatures of the desert.

"They didn't knock me out when I was brought down here." She said softly. She gripped Tempest's hand, "I'm Alice, you just let me help." She pulled her towards Vlad and the door.

"Vlad, you travel in the middle. Jason, take up the rear. Girls, we have to move quickly and quietly. We don't want to be recaptured." They moved silently through the halls. True to her word, Alice lead them up to the stables.

Tempest gasped, looking everywhere at once. There were magnificent lizards. The smallest was the size of an elephant. There were eggs lining one wall, under heat lamps. The wagons were stored against another wall. The two remaining walls were lined with large stables. "OK, get as many as you can on those lizards." Tempest pointed to a pair of bearded dragons. "The rest of you, load up in the wagons." She had become quite the general. Vlad went over to their bags, which were laying against one wall. He quickly put on his sun suit. He gave Tempest a thumbs up before helping to load the girls.

Jason nodded his approval. He opened one of the stables, pulling out one of the lizards. He hooked up one of the wagons. Alice dragged Tempest to the doors and they swung them open. They went to the wagons, loading in with the others. Jason and Vlad took the reins, leading the pair of bearded dragons. Each pulled a wagon out into daylight. Vlad wore his sunsuit and a cloak. Through the cloak, smoke curled upwards slowly, his suit was starting to wear thin in some places. One of the girls, a dingo, went to help Jason. She gave directions to one of their villages. Vlad eventually came down, resting in the wagon, under a canopy. They rode throughout the day.

CHAPTER 19

OASIS

TEMPEST SAT IN THE WAGON, ALICE still clinging to her. They were traveling in the right direction, according to her gut. They arrived in a small village, at dusk. The village was a series of tents, the colour of sand. Dismounting, they left the wagons. The golden eyed people ran towards the village, yelling. Jason, Vlad and Tempest stood with a yeti and what Tempest had been told were a pair of coyotes, an ogre and even a few lizard girls from other parts of the desert. All had been captured. The rest were a part of the dingo race, like Alice.

Alice came back out of the mass of people. She gripped Tempest's hand. Alice pulled her to a bald old man, his furless ears twitching. He leaned heavily on his staff, wrapped in a sand coloured cloak. His skin had been scared by the wind and sandstorms. "Granddad this is Tempest and her traveling companions Vladamire, of the vampire race, and Jason, of the werewolves. They saved us from the reptos" she smiled.

The stooped old man came gripped Tempest's jaw, bringing her down to his level. Staring into her eyes. "Human, Alice are you sure this human saved you?" He asked turning her head. Alice laughed, "yes Granddad. I'm sure she saved us all."

He released her, "then she and her friends will be our honoured guests at supper tonight." He said smiling, "we have much to talk about. But first, the celebration of your rescue!" He shouted the word celebration. The village sprang into action. Golden eyed people running, in what appeared to be utter chaos. Tempest stood watching, in the centre of a cyclone of activity.

Alice dragged them into one of the tents with her grandfather. "We will see to the others. We will take them home. If there is anything we could do, to thank you, please let us know." He told them.

Jason smiled. "Thank you sir, for returning the others to their homes. We could use supplies, to get us through the remainder of this desert. I'll give you a list of details." He slipped out of the tent. He had been acting distant the whole trip from the reptos. Vlad took the opportunity, of being out of the sunlight, to rid himself of his cloak. His suit had several rips in the fabric. He took the suit off. Under it, he wore a T-shirt and shorts. His skin tanned where the fabric had thinned. As he stood there, his skin paled. "I could use some thread or a new suit. I have to repair my sunsuit."

The old man looked at Tempest. "You must be tired. Please rest. Vladamire, we will find you thread and a needle, and perhaps some patches." He headed out, motioning for Alice to follow. "Tempest, we will talk at the party." He left, heading out to supervise the celebrations.

Vlad threw himself on a bed of blankets, "Tempest come on you need rest." He said watching her. Tempest nodded absently. "Don't you have to drink?" She watched the predator, as a dingo dropped off thread and a needle.

He nodded, taking the thread. He started repairing his sunsuit. "Yes, but you had a long couple days and you helped save a group of people." He shook his head, "I'm sure you will find a way to save my life and escape your bond to me. Have a night off Tempest." Vlad saying this to her, was the nicest thing the vampire had said. He finished his repairs and laid down.

Tempest sat down on the blanket bed, then put her head on his shoulder. "Thanks Vlad." She muttered softly, pulling a light sheet over herself. She drifted off to sleep, resting. Her dreams terrorized her, by all manor of creatures, and of being captured as the girls had been. She woke shaking. Vlad sat at the end of the bed speaking softly to Jason. She slowly sat up, watching them. "Guys enough secrets, what's up?" Vlad shot her a glare, as though warning Tempest to stay out of it.

Jason on the other hand was smiling like a love sick puppy. Tempest shook her head. "We have a quest to complete, people to save, remember?" Jason nodded, looking disappointed. Vlad, on the other hand, looked pleased. "What is going on Jason?" She demanded watching the pair.

Vlad sighed, running a hand through his hair. He looked exasperated. "Tempest, Coyotes, Dingos and Wolves are all decedents of the-"

She cut in, "the wolf mother yes, yes I know." She tapped the side of her head. Jason seemed to be growing increasingly nervous, as time went on.

"Tempest, for Dingos, part of their celebration… it has to do with phero- mones the females release. Jason has no control over this, though he's affected by them." Vlad stared at his friend, scratching his own head. "It makes them relax and party."

She shook her head concerned for her friends, "and it doesn't effect you Vlad?" He grinned, "I'm a vampire, not a wolf or a split of the species." Tempest continued, "so Jason just has to get away from here. Then we get the old Jason back, or wait for the party to end?"

Vlad shook his head, "this party can last as long as a month and he won't leave till it ends." He looked worried at Jason.

She sighed, "why is nothing ever easy? So what do you suggest Vlad?" She didn't really want to know what he was thinking, from the glint in his eyes. Vlad looked at Jason. "We just have to override the the pheromones." Tempest nodded following his train of thought. Vlad looked at Jason then held out his hand to take hers.

Tempest reluctantly put her hand in his, then felt a stab of pain. She wrenched her hand back. "What was that for?" She demanded glaring. She clutched her hand to her chest, as it dripped blood from a small cut on her palm.

Vlad looked at her sheepishly, "forgot to say it'll hurt. Sorry Tempest, we just needed to give him another scent to focus on." Tempest shook her head, glaring at Vlad, "why not you?"

"When will you learn, Tempest? As a human, from the outside world, you are special. Your blood contains proteins that he's not used to." Cold logic in his voice.

Jason was sneezing, shaking his head. It was as though he had put pepper up his nose. "What was that for? Feels like I've had my nose burned out!" His hand going to rub the bridge of his nose, he sneezed again and again. She chuckled, "the smell is my blood. Jason we needed to snap you back to your senses."

He shook his head, "I had forgotten that was part of the dingos celebra- tions." He smiled. "I'd love to stick around the Dingo village longer. If it's all right with you guys, I'm gonna go request supplies. What do we need? Any suggestions?"

"We'll we need three days worth of supplies, to get us to the waterfall. After that, a couple hours up river, to a rock arch. From there, I'm hopping for more directions." Tempest didn't know where they were going after that.

"I'll go Jason. I'm not effected by them, like you are. You stay with Tempest and rest." He told Jason, getting to his feet. He glanced over, "Tempest keep him here and don't let that cut close." Vlad instructed before leaving the tent, he was worried. Tempest looked at Jason, "I don't know where we are going after the arch." She felt hopeless.

He sighed, "Tempest, look we will find the lake and fix what's wrong. Even out here, in the desert, they have seen skeletons." Jason pulled her into a hug. "We will get you home, don't worry."

She nodded hopping, he was right. Ten minutes later, Vlad came back. "We've got a ride as far as the waterfall. We move out after supper. They will load our stuff while we eat. Tempest, give me your hand." Vlad pulled her up. "Come on Jason, let's go. They said they will try to stay away from you, for your own good."

CHAPTER 20

LAST MEAL

J ASON NODDED, CLIMBING CLUMSILY TO HIS feet. Vlad moved to steady him. "Tempest, take the other side. It's like being drunk, as far as I can understand it." He told her as they went out to a table. Alice's granddad, and Alice were sitting down at one table. Alice got up and brought them over to sit with him. Vlad glared at her as she sat next to Jason. "I thought we agreed no girls, Merck, Jason is effected by the pheromones."

Alice glared at Vlad. "I'm to young and injured to participate in clan activities." She was angry. "I'll have you know, as the next in line, it's my job to attend meetings. Dinning with guests is another honour." She told them proudly. Vlad nodded as food was brought to them. It was much the same sort of food Jason's people ate, only it was desert creatures cooked. Gazelles and desert hares. When they finished eating, Alice lead them to the wagon, which was hooked to a bearded dragon.

Alice climbed up the lizards neck to steer, while they rode in the wagon. "Now this is the way to travel!" Tempest laughed, leaning on a pile of blankets and pillows. Jason chuckled, "yea I guess this is good!" He smiled. Even Vlad seemed to be in a good mood. He sat in a corner, writing in a journal. He looked up and smiled before going back to his writing.

At dawn the next day, they could see mountains approaching. By noon, they had arrived at a trickling stream. As they traveled, the stream became a river. Tempest climbed up, ridding with Alice, on the bearded dragon's head. They were traveling faster than she had anticipated.

The waterfall came into view in the approaching mountain. Tempest let out a whoop of laughter, they were almost there. She climbed down, getting the supplies from the wagon. Alice hugged them, before waving and heading off back, into the desert. They walked up to the falls. It was two hundred meters straight up. Water poured over the top, crashing in front of them, into a lake, leading to the river they had followed. There was a rock wall. Next to the waterfall, plants grew on the wall. This provided something for them to hang onto. Tempest shook her head "we have to go up, any ideas?"

Vlad nodded pulling a grappling hook and rope from his pack. "I got this, don't worry, up we go." He threw the hook, the rope trailing behind as it flew. Vlad practically flew up the wall. Jason climbed, with Tempest clinging to his back. When they reached the top, they saw a river running to the falls. All around were trees and wildlife. It seemed more alive than it had anywhere else Tempest had ever seen. They walked up the river, until they reached a stone arch, standing between trees.

CHAPTER 21

END OF THE ROAD

T EMPEST STARED AT THE ARCH BEFORE walking to it. She walked around tapping the sides. Nothing happened, but the hooks were pulling her here, to this exact spot. She walked through it. Whoosh.... the forest vanished. She was engulfed by a white light. She was in another forest, next to a large lake. All around the lake were skeletons, walking around stumbling, moving and hunting. Tempest backed through the arch. Another flash of light and she was back with Jason and Vlad. "We have a problem guys. The lake is surrounded by skeletons." She filled them in on what she had seen at the lake. Jason ran to her, checking her arms for wounds, while asking, "did any of them touch you?" Tempest shook her head, "no I wasn't seen."

Vlad sat down heavily. "Well, I guess that's it. Quest over, we don't stand a chance against an army of skeletons."

Tempest looked at the guys, defeated. They were so close. "Look we can't just give up. Everyone's depending on us. If this is where magic goes wrong, then there must be a way to fix it! I don't get to go home otherwise. You and all your people, will be infected and turned into skeletons. What happens when it mutates and enters my world? Then what?" She demanded staring at them.

Jason just stared at her, "damn your right. Okay, what do we know about these creatures?"

Vlad gave him a look that said, 'you've got to be joking' before stating: "fire, they are destroyed using fire and are afraid of fire. However, fire could destroy the lake and the trees. Which would probably destroy magic, and kill us."

Tempest nodded, "so controlled fire. Let's sleep on it and see what we can dream up. I'll take first watch." She turned to face the arch. Jason and Vlad didn't bother with sleeping gear. They sat with their backs to the trees, weapons in hand.

A third of the night through, Tempest woke Jason. An hour before dawn, Vlad woke them excitedly. "I've got it! I go through and cut a fire break. Jason and you use arrows on fire or fire swords and we control the fires." Jason shook his head, "we would be over run. What we need, is a fire storm." He looked at Vlad, who's face darkened as Jason spoke. "Vlad think about it!" He said frustratedly.

"No way, not happening. You almost burnt up the last time, Jason!" Vlad was horrified by the idea of a fire storm.

Tempest looked at Jason "what's a fire storm?" She looked between the pair of them before demanding angrily, "no secrets!"

Jason grinned proudly, "a fire storm, is a storm made with the help of fire elementals. Combined with air and a bit of water. I'm one of the few capable of controlling it."

Vlad snorted, "barely. The last time he conjured one, he almost died!" He watched Jason, who was concentrating on a ball of fire in his hands. "This is a fire storm." In the centre the eye, stood a small figure. Outside his protective bubble a storm of fire raged. "If we were to use that, we could incinerate the skeletons." He smiled like he had solved the whole problem. It would keep the fire from the lake and trees.

Vlad shook his head, "and when you burn up in fiery glory, what then?"

"My people would be safe, as would the rest of the people. We stop the skeletons who are contaminating the water. I'm sure the rest will ether be cured or killed. Does it matter what happens to me, if the people are safe?"

"Yes, it matters. You have a clan to rule, and people to care for. People who care for you." Tempest said softly.

He shook his head "but those people would be safe, and theres no guarantee I'd burn up."

"No, Jason we will find another way." Vlad admitted, "we will keep the fire storm as a back up plan. If we can think of something else, before noon, we won't have to use it."

Jason only nodded absently, "Tempest, where were you spat out by the arch?" She drew the lake on the ground and added an X, to represent the portal off to one side. "It was surrounded by trees," she said shivering. "But, the lake was surrounded by them." She explained the layout. Jason and Vlad nodded, "if we used the firestorm, how would we stop them from scrambling?" Vlad sighed, "we would need bait. Jason would need his strength, he's ruled out. They have no interest in me. Tempest that leaves you, you would have to be bait."

Tempest nodded, "okay, any other ideas to beat the skeletons?" She started to make lunch for them. They racked their brains for another solution. As noon approached, they came to realize, there was no other way. They had to do this. They had to use Jason and the fire storm. "OK, I'm bait got it...how do I become bait?" She asked as they ate the last of the supplies.

Vlad looked at her, "well, you are human. That's bait enough. You and I will go through the portal, drawing in as many skeletons to the lake as possible. I act as your body guard. Jason, you will come after us." He checked his weapons. "Tempest you wear shorts, and a T-shirt. Jason, give us five minutes. Once they gather, Jason, you start the fire storm. Tempest you hide in the water."

Jason nodded and clapped his hands together. "OK, let's go." They got ready to go. They left all the gear they could behind them except, for their weapons. Vlad made sure all their weapons were sharp. They walked to the portal and ran through, heading straight for the lake. They ran as fast as they could, the skeletons sensing them, surround them. Standing at the lake, they waited. The skeletons gathered around, lunging at her. When enough of the skeletons gathered around the lake, Vlad shoved her into the water. He dove in after her. It was only waist deep. They sat, as Jason came through, burning the skeletons towards the lake. Jason came closer to the lake, standing with his back to them. Jason had flames flying out of his hands, surrounding him. He expanded the fire outwards, towards the skeletons. They watched as the flames incinerated the skeletons. The bones blackening, crackling and rattling. Vlad gripped Jason's leg, getting ready to pull him in and shut the storm down by force, if Jason lost control.

Vlad's hand smouldered and blackened from the heat. When the last skeleton was incinerated, Vlad didn't even wait for Jason. He pulled him directly into the water. The suit around Vlad's hand, had flames licking their way up his arms. Tempest pulled Vlad, who pulled Jason under the water. The sun high above them. Jason spluttered water as he surfaced. He looked at Vlad, his suit had been burnt from touching Jason. He cradled his burnt hand to his chest, smoke curling upwards from him. Tempest tore Jason's shirt off, wrapping it around Vlad's hand pulling him into the shade of a nearby tree.

The water had been a sickly green, but as Tempest watched, the water turned blue, spreading from where they had been. "Jason, Vlad we did it!" She cheered as she helped Vlad into the shadows, projected by some trees. "You okay there Vlad?" She heard a groan from him. Jason went to the side of the lake, watching the water clean itself. He went back, through the arch, fetching their supplies. Jason soon returned, with their bags. When the water finished clearing, a merman swam up to them from deep within the water. "Thank you for clearing the skeletons out." He had long red hair that went down his back. His bright blue eyes stared at them. "It is in my power to send you where you need to be or grant you a wish."

Jason nodded, "the vampires mansion. Send us to the vampire mansion, please." There was a flash of light, they were transported to the main room in the vampires mansion. Eric walked into the room, straightening Vlad up gently. He helped his slightly cooked son. He looked at Jason and Tempest, "Tempest are you the one who did this?" He asked rage filling his voice.

Tempest nodded. Jason stood at her shoulder, watching over her. He put an arm around her shoulders protectively. "She saved my life, now she's going home." Vlad told his father. Eric dusted Vlad off, examining his arm. "She saved me from being burnt worse then I was."

Eric nodded, "fine. Jason get her out of here, before Orben catches her scent."

Jason nodded and lead her out. They headed towards his camp. "It's almost fall, my people will be traveling to the city again." He smiled softly as they walked. Several days later, they reached the camp. They found that everyone had already moved on to the city.

Jason sighed, "I'll walk you back to the line." He lead her through the abandoned camp site, through the forest, back to the park. The birds had remained frozen in mid air. She walked up to the barrier. As she passed through, the birds unfroze. The wind started moving in the trees. "If you ever need me, I'll be there. When you wish to see Emor, just come find me. I'll be around. There are many ways to get into my world."

Tempest looked at Jason, "I guess this is goodbye." He nodded and looked over her head. Her world awaited. She took one step further, then looked back at Jason, he was gone, as though he had never been. Almost as though, it had been her own imagination, a dream. She looked at her wrist, the paw print still there. She smiled. It hadn't been a dream, she knew that.

Tempest walked to where she had left her bike, she unlocked it, looking towards the sky. The birds were flying, time had unfrozen. The sun seemed brighter, the sky was bluer. Even the air felt cleaner. She took a deep breath. It was defiantly cleaner. Tempest knew then, that by helping save magic, she'd helped heal her own world, if only a little bit. She collected her bike and headed home. She biked as fast as she could. When she reached the door, she threw it open. Tempest ran in, not bothering to put her bike away. Her parents were just waking up. The coffee maker barely heated. "Hi mum, hi dad!" She hugged them, she was home. She smiled, her mind drifting to her diary. She looked forward to the fact that soon, she would be writing her story down.

"What did you do to your ankle?" She heard her older brother Steve ask, as he came out of the bathroom. His brown hair wet from the shower. She shrugged, smiling at her family. "Good morning to you to." Before heading off to her room, to write her diary.

PART 2
THE CALLING

CHAPTER 1

RETURN

A MONTH HAD PASSED, SINCE TEMPEST HAD helped save magic, with Vlad and Jason. Life had begun to feel so slow, so normal. It was hard to believe, the amazing adventure she had participated in. She shook her head, staring at herself in the bathroom mirror. Her eyes had returned to blue-grey, except for the occasional flash of green. She watched for it or thought of magic and saw the colour flash. Her mother had cut her hair, telling her she needed a new style for school. Now it was short, wispy and ALWAYS in her way! Tempest turned, leaving the washroom. Her finger tracing the wolf print on her wrist. Most of the time, it was faded out barely visible. If she thought about it, it appeared, as bright as the day she had received it. She stumbled over her backpack, picking it up. She glanced inside. This sitting still was killing her. She had her daggers that Vlad had given her. Along with some granola bars, a change of clothes and a bottle of water.

The last week had been the longest of her life. Each day she got up, and ate breakfast with her parents and brother. She spent the time her family was at work, playing video games and watching T.V. The time they were home she hung out, enjoying the time with them.

However, the slow life could never last. For the first time in weeks she yelled from her room, "I'm going biking." It was the weekend, so everyone was home. It couldn't hurt to blow off steam, could it? She'd simply go to the park and look around. She pocketed her compass, putting her bag on as she grabbed her helmet. Tempest ran to the garage, pulling her bike out from behind it. She jumped on, peddling straight to the park. As she hit the grass, she didn't slow, didn't stop, the tree line flew past. She biked deeper, determined to find Jason and her next adventure. As she hit the abandoned camp site, she remembered they had gone to Emor for the winter. "East, the city lies east." She turned east. She thought about the air challenge, flying over the great city. The spiral towers, the clouds, the creatures, the cobbled streets, the magic, and the adventure of it all.

It was time to see what she could do. She stopped at the wolves camp site and got off her bike. Going to the storage hut, she placed her hand on the door. The paw print on her wrist glowed bright green, unlocking the door. She went inside stuffing some jerky and supplies into her bag. On the shelf next to the jerky, was a card about the size of a business card. On it was written 'for Tempest.' She flipped it over, expecting a note. What she found was a map. On the top there was writing in a strange script. "English is the only language I know." She watched the script shimmer, the shifting script now read 'how may I help?' She dropped the card in surprise and it went blank. Slowly, she picked it up again. 'World of magic' appeared above the map. The map labeled with all the places she had been and many more. A small blue dot hovered over a label that read, 'Wolf Summer Camp.' "Does this thing zoom?" Tempest asked, nothing happened. "Magnify please." She said aloud, thinking perhaps another command would work. Instantly there was a map of the village, with a blue dot on a building labeled Supply House.

Tempest grinned, "thanks Jason. Map to Emor please." She was being polite in case the paper was sentient. Who knew with this magic stuff? The map card displayed a green line, leading her out of the supply house and to the east. She smiled. She had been right, east was the way to go. She left the supply house a bag of wooden figurines tossed into her bag. She pocketed the map card, climbing on her bike, she headed east. When it was nearing dusk, she set up camp. She remembered helping Jason set up camp every night they traveled. It was as though he had been training her for her return. She pulled out the bag of figurines, taking the wooden miniature carving of the tent. It fit in the palm of her hand. Jason had taught her enough magic to use these figurines.

She set it on the ground, closing her eyes. "Enlarge." She concentrated. A few moments later she peeked from one eye. Letting out a whoop of joy, she jumped into the air. It had worked on her first try. Before her stood a full size, one person tent. It was a vibrant pink, instead of a green or brown, but she could live with that. Gathering some dry bark and twigs, she cleared the ground in front of the tent. She enlarged a small shovel from the figurines and dug a shallow crater. She set the twigs, leaves and bark in a teepee formation, before pulling out the fire stick from her bag. Tempest put the fire end in the bark and leaves. "Light" She said concentrating on warmth, heat and light, just as Jason taught her.

She smelt wood smoke, grinning she put the stick and shovel away again. Her hands warmed over the small fire. It was a welcome companion, for the cold air that came with the late summer night. She looked up as the first stars of the night started to appear over head. Memories of nights spent camping with Vlad and Jason. Learning the stars names. It all came flooding back to her. A tear fell from her eye. Wiping it away, she realized she missed them. They were almost family, if a vampire and a werewolf could be family. She sat back, leaning against a nearby tree, watching the stars before she went into the tent.

She zipped the door shut and lay down. She hadn't bothered with a sleeping bag, knowing she would be warm enough within the tent. She had minutes before the fire would die out. The light from the dying embers danced on the walls before going dark. She closed her eyes, and with that she fell asleep, the forest sounds around her providing an accompaniment to sleep by.

CHAPTER 2

EMOR

S HE WOKE TO BIRD SONGS AND the wind rustling through the leaves. Leaving the tent and going to the front, she shrunk it back to the small wooden figurine. She picked it up, placing it back within it's bag. She walked through the trees with her bike, following the map card and her compass. It was going on noon when the spires and towers appeared. They pointed up through the trees ahead of her. Small dots appeared, soaring around the towers. As she came closer, the small dots changed into gryphons and dragons. She walked on, seeing the vibrant colours of the towers and creatures flashing in the sunlight. At the edge of the trees, the city of Emor lay before her in a basin. Walking down, she approached slowly. Walls surrounded the city, though they were only hip high. She avoided climbing them, however, as the map pointed for her to go around to the front gates. It looked as though they were decorative stone walls covered in swirling patterns. She walked down the basin side, towards the city. Most of the houses were old homes. They looked as though they belonged in a small ancient hamlet. As she approached the city, the dirt changed to cobbled stone paths. The grass everywhere was neatly trimmed, everything orderly and immaculate. She walked through the gate, following the path inside. The city was truly a wonder, there were no cars or telephone poles. No electric lighting, but old light posts lit with flames danced even in the daylight. Fountains lay everywhere, decorating the streets. Baskets of flowers hung from most of the buildings. Murals were painted on many of the walls, depicting different historical points.

She stood still for a moment, just taking in the sights. She gazed around herself and pulled the card from her pocket. "Could you please lead me to Jason?" She asked the map. Instantly, scrawling appeared, 'welcome to Emor' then it magnified to where Tempest stood. The map now included a blue dot, that was Tempest. A green line lead from her to a stationary red dot. Tempest grinned, walking through the arches. She past magnificent columns, everywhere she looked there were carvings, murals and statues. Everything was painted in bright colours, decorating the magnificent city.

There were new sights all around. A new impossibility. Like the fountains, each one seemed to do something different. She stopped to stare at a few of them. There were a few that had water like fountains in her own world, others blew coloured bubbles. Some blew liquid rainbows, pouring into the bottom. She shook her head. This place was an impossibility and she was loving every moment.

Looking back at her map, she chuckled. She felt amazingly happy, almost complete. She glanced at the map and walked down the street. The streets were filled with people of every sort. There were lion people with manes around their faces and tails swishing. Lizard people, werewolves and vampires. There were creatures she couldn't even begin to guess what species they belonged to. She shook her head in utter disbelief, as she walked towards a huge white marble building. Stone steps lead up to the massive double doors. It was guarded by a pair of life-size stone gryphons, with columns marching across the front of the building. It made an impressive sight. The red dot showed that this was the place she wanted. She reached the building, going up the imposing stone steps. A label on the map appeared, 'Library.' She grinned. Where else would she find Jason, researching and working. She walked in and was stunned to find herself in a hallway lined with lockers. They didn't seem to have locks, they were tied shut with bits of coloured string. Tempest walked through the hall, down towards the red dot on the map. The map had changed to show the library floor plan. She was in a locker room according to the map. Ahead was the library. She walked through the door and let out a gasp. To say the room was filled with books, was putting it lightly. There were more books there than she had ever seen in her life.

CHAPTER 3

REUNION

HE BUILDING HAD LOOKED RECTANGULAR, FROM the outside. On the inside, however, it was circular like a silo, though much wider. She looked up. High above her was a skylight. She looked down beneath her feet. On the floor, in tiles was a map of the world. It wasn't the world she knew. The geography was forming different continents. There were six floors visible from where she was standing. There were far more above those, each rimmed the room. Everywhere she looked, there were people wearing black robes. Some had strips of colour around the hoods, hems and sleeves. She looked down at the map it said that Jason was on this floor. Around the side, sitting at one of the tables, littered around the room haphazardly. As the map fed her directions, she walked until she was a shelf away from Jason. Once there, she pocketed the map. She peeked through the books on the shelf. There sat Jason, his back to her. Vlad was sitting across from him. They were both surrounded by books on the table, but were playing chess. Both wore the black robes with the hoods down. Obviously, not studying. She approached, motioning for Vlad to stay silent. Her finger across her lips. She leaped at Jason, "BOO!" Jason literally bounced, jumping up. He turned around, lifting her off the ground. He spun her around and set her back down on her feet.

"What are you doing here Tempest?" Jason asked hands landing heavily on her shoulders.

Tempest smiled as Vlad got up and stood next to Jason. They were the same hight, though that was where the similarities ended. Jason had his dark green eyes and dark hair. While Vlad had his bright red eyes, blond hair and shockingly pale skin. "Well, you see, this guy I knew offered to show me his city and school. He neglected to pick me up. So, I had to find my own way here." Jason ruffled her hair smiling down at her.

"Yes, well I thought you had had enough of my world. You just wanted to go home." Jason teased her. "So what do you want to see first?"

Tempest shrugged, "the real world is a bit...slow. It's almost the fall. My parents are at work, my brother is at work a lot and well I'm bored!" She said exasperated. It really had become predictable, in the normal human world. "Not to mention, how slow school is going to be when I go back."

Vlad laughed, "well I think we can show you the schools and introduce you to Raven. We should also ask Rhydian to make a portal for you. Tempest. If you plan to visit us more often, I can only imagine how long a walk it was to get here. Come on Jason, take her around the city. We can take her to Raven later, and show her the school."

Jason nodded, "Vlad can you go get Rhydian started on a portal. We will go talk to the headmistress of the schools, Raven, after I show her a bit of the city." Vlad closed the books that had been laying around, packing up before he left.

Jason nodded again, "alright, how about we go see the wolves at the winter camp?" He suggested, "as it is our winter camp, it's a bit more permanent." Jason lead her back through the locker hall. He pulled his robe off, over his head, revealed jeans and a T-shirt. "Only have to wear it in the library." He threw the robe in one locker labeled Jason. His backpack was inside. He grabbed it and placed it on his shoulders. Waving his hand over the lock spot, thread wove out and tied it shut. "Each building has a separate dress code. The library, black robes. The Nest, that's the flight school, requires a flight suit. Advanced magic school tower requires rubber shoes. However, we are going to my home, no dress code required." He lead her out through the city streets, to the outer edges of town. "Each species has it's own embassy, here on the outskirts of Emor. This is mine. Walk into these trees, follow the wolves laws." They walked into the trees, before them lay a huge log lodge.

CHAPTER 4

WOLF LODGE

TEMPEST CHUCKLED, "A LITTLE MORE PERMANENT eh?" He laughed as he lead her up to the door. "Only people with wolf blood or friends of wolves may enter." The wood was covered in carvings of wolves most of it was history. Tempest nodded, "like the huts?" He smiled and she placed her hand on the door next to his. The door rose slowly into the ceiling, when it finished rising, Jason lead her into the house.

"The main floor are the living quarters. The next two are the sleeping quarters, and the top floor is the playroom for the kids who aren't in school yet." He lead her through the kitchen, his mother, Jessica, and some other people were cooking. Her hair was as dark as Jason's. Her eyes just as green as his. She looked a lot better than when Tempest had last seen her. Healing magic had healed his people, as well as Tempest's own world.

In the middle of the kitchen there was a large island with a ton of chairs around it. Sitting around it a group of people worked on the next meal. "Hey Tempest, how are you?" Jessica called as Jason lead her through the kitchen.

"I"m good! Nice to see you!" She called back as she was lead past the living room. It looked more like a green house. Herbs grew everywhere in pots, on the arms of the couches, on the backs of the couches, on the wall shelves and on piles of books.

Jason lead her upstairs, past the sleeping quarters, to the playroom. Scott's little brother Ethan wandered from a group of kids, going to Jason "Scott hasn't come home from school yet." He looked like a much younger version of Scott, only short and pudgy.

Jason nodded looking around "when was he supposed to come back?" He asked looking concerned.

Ethan held up two fingers, "this many hours ago."

Jason nodded, "I'll ask around. Ethan, stay here with your sister." He lead Tempest to the front wall. The room resembled a kindergarden class room. Tables and art supplies lay around, with picture books. The front wall had a hole leading to a slide that curled around.

Tempest got in, sliding down and around. It spat them out on the main floor, in the living room. Jason went into the kitchen to his mother. "Have you seen Scott?" She heard him ask, Tempest stayed in the living room, waiting for Jason. He came back looking worried. "Let's go show you the school and introduce you to Raven. The school is mandatory, everyone goes. This is required to foster peace. I'll take a look for Scott, while we are there." They left the wolf lodge as he continued to talk. "The school requires a backpack, with pens and paper. Good ears don't hurt either, and clean clothes." He smiled, "oh and a hat that tells where your dorm room is, what school you are in or what your practice is."

Tempest raised her eyebrow, "and where is your hat?" He rummaged through his bag, bringing out a green baseball hat. On the front was a black gryphon.

He pulled it on, over his black hair. "Colour for species, gryphon for where I study. There are dorms located within each school of study. If I were to sleep within my dorms, I'd be in the building that looks like a tree. The Nest is the flight school." He pointed to a large tree shaped tower. They walked down the cobble stone street, towards the tower, with the planets rotating around it.

"Magic school?" Tempest asked, watching them rotate around the tower.

He nodded, "yes, that is the main magic building. The head of the three schools also has her office there. You have to complete magic school basics before choosing another field to study. Like Vlad. He's studying at the Advanced Magic School, AMS for short. I, however, am going to the Nest. The magic students, who choose to carry on their studies, go to the AMS." He explained everything. It was a little overwhelming. "The guard are made from both those who fly and those who graduate from AMS. We share the responsibility of protecting this world."

CHAPTER 5

ATTACK SQUIRRELS AND MARSHMALLOWS

"WHO IS RHYDIAN?" TEMPEST STARED UP at the tower they were walking towards. The planets rotated as they spun slowly around the tower. Somehow all nine avoided each other. She noticed all the little moons, floating around them, moving on their own. Amazing, simply amazing she thought to herself.

"Rhydian is a good friend who can get magic to do just about anything. He is our magic techno geek. Magic impossibilities are his speciality." They reached the courtyard surrounding the tower.

The courtyard was guarded by a stone wall, knee high. Jason continued around, toward the gate. She looked at him, "why don't we just jump the wall?"

He shook his head, "jump the wall if you dare." He grinned. Tempest looked at the wall and stepped over. Instantly, mini rainbow marshmallows were flying at her. She looked in the direction they were coming from, high in a tree. The tree was growing marshmallows. High in the branches, sat little chipmunks and squirrels, throwing marshmallows at her! She leaped back to the other side of the wall, where Jason was howling with laughter.

Tempest stomped over to him and hit his shoulder. "Attack squirrels? What do you guys do around here, find the most impossible thing and make it possible?" Shaking her head, as he continued laughing.

"Yes," he choked as he laughed. "Marshmallow trees are the best."

They walked to the gate and then onto a dirt path. "Why aren't they attacking now?" She brushed marshmallows from her hair. He smiled at her, turning, he helped pull marshmallows out of her hair.

"You entered the right way, before you were on their nuts."

"Their nuts?" She asked utterly confused.

He nodded, "they are buried all over the place. Everywhere but the path." He smiled at her. He took a marshmallow, and popped it into his mouth. "There's a group of flyers who specialize in speaking to animals. The squirrels love to talk. We talked them into having all this space to burry nuts in, as long as they avoided the path." Jason admitted. A squirrel held a marshmallow out to her, chattering away. "Better then having the city infested, they have their space."

She looked at Jason "what's he saying?"

Jason laughed, "he's apologizing for the marshmallows and offering peace."

Tempest grinned, taking the marshmallows. "Thanks." She ate the marshmallow quickly. "I'll stay off the grass, if I can eat marshmallows." The squirrel nodded and then took off running into the trees. They walked to the front door. It wasn't a grand door, just a standard slab of wood, no knob or handle just wood.

Jason put his hand on the door, "open please, we are here to see the headmistress, Raven." The door swung open. A green line appeared on the wall, displaying the route to the headmistresses office. Jason lead her through the hallways. They were covered in tapestries, displaying magical spells in action. These were far from your traditional tapestries. They were on woven cloth, however, they were done as comic book strips. Complete with words like 'pow' and 'zap'. Down the hallway they came to a doorway. The door stood wide open, unlike most of the other doors, which were firmly closed.

Inside was a desk and a table, covered in maps with little clay figures. A women stood watching the figures, her back to the doorway. Purple hair hung down to her waist. She was dressed in jeans and a T-shirt. She didn't look anything like a headmistress of a school, let alone headmistress of all the schools here or a warlord. As she turned around, they saw her T-shirt was an old rock and roll shirt - ACDC. Tempest grinned in amusement. If this was the headmistress, school here must be awesome. Her purple eyes bore into Tempests, observing her.

"Jason what are you doing in my office? Tell me you didn't get into another fight, or that you didn't skydive off AMS again." She sounded exasperated.

Jason chuckled, "no ma'am. In fact, this time I'm not even here for me. I'm here for Tempest. She's the human who helped Vlad and I save magic. I told her I'd show her around, if we survived. Here we are alive and well, so I owe her." He smiled his charming smile.

She nodded, "human, I think there's one still living here in the city. Most have moved on to other settlements, or have gone home." She smiled as though she knew a secret. "Well Tempest, I'm the headmistress, Raven. Usually, people only get to see me if they are in trouble. Seeing as your not in trouble, please have a seat." She gestured to a couch against one wall. Tempest sat down as instructed, while Jason dropped down on the soft cushy couch, next to her. It was almost like being back on the clouds. "Do you wish to learn magic?" Raven waved her hand. A cup of tea floated to her. "It's not an easy thing to learn for a human. Though there have been several who have made a name for themselves, both here and in your own world. People such as Harry Houdini and Robert Houdini and of course the mysterious Dante."

"I understand, but I need to know what I can do." Tempest admitted. She looked at Jason, he was just smiling, pride filled his eyes. She knew she had said the right thing to impress him and the headmistress.

Raven nodded, "then I have some questions for you. Are you going to want to live in the human world or this one?"

"Human if possible." Tempest said, smiling as Raven's cup of tea landed perfectly balanced in her hand.

"I take it you already have Rhydian working on a portal?" Raven asked Jason who nodded. She looked back at Tempest. "You will need a room, to store things here and a place to come through. New students are required to keep a strict sleep schedule and health routine. We will be keeping watch, monitoring you. There can be disastrous results for a human who takes up magic. Will you want a dorm room here at the school, or are you going to have a space at the wolf house?"

Tempest grinned, "I wouldn't mind one here, and I'll keep to the rules." She was determined to learn whatever they would teach her.

Raven nodded, "good. We have an opening on the twelfth floor. I believe that would do. Jason, if you would take her for supplies in the store room,

I believe Rhydian will have the portal done by now. Your room is on the twelfth floor, room eight." She dismissed them with a wave of her hand.

CHAPTER 6

RHYDIAN'S HOUSE OF TECH

J ASON LEAD TEMPEST TO A STAIRCASE next to the staircase was a pile of rugs. "Floor three please." He asked as he picked up one of the rugs and placed it on the foot of the stairs. The rug spun them up until they hit the third floor. As the rug stopped they stepped off the rug and laid it back on the pile. He lead her down the hallway. They walked into the storage room, which looked like a huge warehouse. Rows of books, supplies, clothes, robes, hats, anything and everything you could think, and some stuff you couldn't. A warehouse of stuff. He grinned, watching the shocked look on Tempest's face. He lead her down the rows of shelves. At the end was a door, which slid open as they reached it.

Inside was a gear-head's dream. There were work benches covered in hammers, screwdrivers, wires, wire cutters, string and every tool you could ever want. Saws, pulleys and screws. There was a sort of organized chaos to it. Then she saw Rhydian. He was humanoid, but a cross between a very angry chameleon and a human. As she watched, his skin ripple with scales. His hair was a fiery red, sticking out in every direction. Tempest smiled. He stood and his tail wrapped tightly around his jean clad legs, which ended in clawed feet. He turned to look at them, goggles lay against his chest. He was covered in a heavy glass-blowers protective apron. He smiled huge teeth showing, his arms opened to hug them.

Jason smiled, "hey Rhydian. How are you?" He looked around the room, "did you clean in here or did they finally give you an assistant to organize?"

Rhydian chuckled, "I'm good and yes they send someone in weekly to clean. This must be Tempest, our little hero!" He came towards them, embracing the pair of them tightly. Tempest noticed bits of wire and string sticking out of his hair. He picked her up, setting her on the work bench. She giggled. "This, Tempest, is your portal maker!" He pulled out a pocket watch from behind her ear, holding it for her to see. He snapped it open and she watched the hands tick. There was an extra knob on the top. It was a beautiful piece of work, with a three masted schooner on the front. Inside, across from the watch face, lay a working compass. "Hit this knob when you are standing in your room upstairs, then hit the same knob in your room in the human world. That sets it. After that, hit it to transport from one space to the other. To reset, double click." He spoke rapidly. "Draw a circle on the ground, in both spaces that way you don't put anything in the space you will appear in. That can be unfortunate and uncomfortable and well complicated to fix. Best to avoid that!'"

"What are you?" Tempest blurted out. She couldn't help it, her curiosity was killing her.

He tweaked her nose. "I, my dear, am a genius or a mad scientist." He let out an infectious laugh, looking her in the eye. "My kind are an ancient race, an off shoot of the dragons. We are the people of the constellation Draco. The decedents of the dragons. I believe you met some of my reptilian cousins, in the deep desert. Distant relations."

She nodded, "not the friendliest bunch." Tempest admitted watching warily. If he was a part of their people, she knew they could be dangerous.

"I know but I am not like them." He smiled, "they chose to go wild. My own people choose to build their minds and culture. Now you guys should get the portal set. Jason, you should go with her and make sure it anchors in her world."

Tempest nodded, she could not wait to start exploring, Rhydian put some papers in a folder, then handed it to her. "If you decide to move here, rather then living in both worlds, there are papers there explaining how to go about it. Also papers on the schools and on Emor." He smiled once again.

Tempest nodded, "thank you" she smiled back. "It mean's a lot that I am welcome." Jason lead her back to the staircase taking another rug up to the twelfth floor. They stepped off, walking down the hall. She saw a door with a number eight on it. Written in green ink was a note saying, 'welcome Tempest' as she read it, the note disappeared by magic.

Jason looked at her, "go on put your hand on the door." Smiling, she put her hand on the door. It swung open, allowing her to see the room. "I'll bring up supplies after we get the portal set in the human world."

She looked at her wrist, "at this rate, this mark will never fade off." She looked at the paw print.

Jason chuckled, "why would you want it to. There is no need for it to, not here. Here it shows what you are, who you are."

"Thanks Jason." She said taking in her room. There was a bunk bed made of wood, a pair of old wooden dressers, a pair of empty book cases and two desks. On each desk was a piece of white chalk. Tempest picked up one and stood in the corner next to the door. She drew a circle large enough for her to stand in comfortably. Then she clicked the watch, it flashed with a bright light from within.

Jason nodded, "okay, let's get the one in your human room set up." He held out a hand. "Come on, it'll be an easy trip. We should be getting you home anyway." Tempest groaned. She didn't want to have to walk all the way back or even bike back.

She looked at Jason, he was laughing. "What?" She asked, looking at him.

"Don't worry, you are in my world now. Transports easy. Come on, I'll show you." With that he lead her from the room. They hopped on a rug and rode down to the ground floor.

Raven was standing in her office, her hands held a purple hat. She threw it through her doorway towards Tempest. Reaching out, catching it, she noticed it had nine planets on the front. She placed it on her head, grinning. It was the start of her next adventure.

Jason lead her out the front doors and into the courtyard. They followed the path to the street. Coming to an old two story style house, an old rounded door swung open as they approached. "You live here?" Tempest asked as they walked in.

"Yes so do Vlad and Rhydian, when he chooses to leave his work rooms. I'm up on the top floor. Vlad is on the main, and Rhydian is the floor beneath the basement. The basement has our kitchen and living room. It's not a bad place for three guys." They stepped onto the staircase and walked up to Jason's floor. The door opened on it's own, revealing a room filled with plants, laundry and hammock that hung from one wall. There were posters of far off places covering the rest. He went over to a bookcase, pulling down a bag. "OK let's go!" They walked back the way they had come and left his house.

Back on the street, Tempest noticed people tended to stare at her, as though she had two heads, which some of them did. "What's their problem?" She asked nervously.

He shook his head, "you'll have to get used to it. It's rare to see a new human. Most have never seen a human from your time period." She sighed, she hated being the centre of attention. Having everyone watch her, just made her skin crawl. Jason lead her to the nest, which appeared to be made from a tree. This was the flight school. Gryphons and dragons soared in and out of the branches.

CHAPTER 7

FIRST FLIGHT

S HE LOOKED AT JASON IN AMAZEMENT, "built or grown?" She spluttered. Leaves fell all around them in many colours, just as the trees in the mortal world were starting into fall colours. He chuckled, "a bit of both actually. The tower, if you don't mind a bit of history was grown by the AMS mages. When we began to communicate with animals, they wanted us to have our own space, to study. The driving force behind it, was a vampire who was frustrated with squirrels burring nuts in his bed and slippers. So he created a plan, the mages grew us a place to study and communicate with all creatures. We were seen as a sort of plague in the magic community for a while!" He admitted, as they walked through an arch to go within the tree.

She looked up high above. She could see dragons and gryphons, leaping above their heads, from perch to perch. The room was crisscrossed with beams. There were no internal walls. There were beams to walk on, and ladders, she shook her head. "This place....it's amazing." A blue dragon soared over their heads, there were so many different types. There were alcoves built into the wall, for people to sleep in. Some were occupied, others were storage ledges.

Jason chuckled, leading her up a myriad of ladders, ledges and beams. He was taking her up the safest way he could, sticking close to the tree wall. Tempest watched as the other people ran across beams, not a hand in width. They wore dark green cargo pants, heavy boots, tank tops and flight jackets. Jason smiled, "home away from home, this is the Nest. We are a sort of military. We protect the magic world, we are the basis for the Guard. When our kind run into your world, or something turns wild, we come in. I work here, when I can...I'll have to give it up when I take over my fathers clan seat. Until then, I spend as much time here as I can. If someone starts a war, we protect and try to sort it out." He was smiling. He was obviously proud of the job he preformed. When they were about halfway up, the inside of the tree, he turned to a cubby hole in the tree. He took out a flight jacket, holding it out to her. She pulled it on, it was a heavy cotton coat, with warm fur on the inside. He then took a spare helmet, plunking it onto her head. It was like a pilots helmet, heavy, he placed the visor down, securing the straps.

Jason pulled a small whistle from his pocket. He put on his own jacket and helmet from the bag, stowing the bag in the cubby. Then blowing the whistle, which made no sound. He looked upwards. His helmet was solid green, a gryphon on ether side. On the back was his name, in black ink. His rank was written above his name, captain. Greyhook, the gryphon from the air challenge, landed in front of them on a small ledge. "Come on," Jason told her. Tempest noticed that his jacket sported a variety of badges. He climbed up. He pulled her onto Greyhook's back, taking her folder and hat. He tucked them into his jacket. Tempest felt him kick gently, then they were off. Tempest wrapped her arms around him, tightly. Falling was not something she wanted to experience. Greyhook flapped his wings, raising them toward the top of the tree. His powerful wings carried them up, through the hollowed tower. They reached an opening at the top. Shooting out through the branches, up into the sky. Tempest gasped, her arms tightening around Jason. She could feel him chuckling.

They soared just above the tree line. All to quickly, they were over his summer camp. Tempest realized they were flying faster than they had during the air challenge. They came to the edge of the trees and over the park. Tempest saw that time wasn't frozen, it was near dusk on the second day. "My parents are going to kill me," she groaned, her shoulders sagging.

"Don't worry," Jason's voice came through the helmet, "I'll take care of it." They soared over the park and into the city. They were lucky, it was almost dusk. They flew unseen above the houses arriving at her parent's place. To her surprise, Greyhook landed on the roof, as light as a feather. Taking off the flight gear on the roof, Jason floated them off the roof, lowering them to the ground. Jason made eye contact with Tempest, "this is going to hurt." He bent down, tapping her ankle. She gasped as she felt the muscles twist.

"What was that for?" She snapped angrily.

"It's an alibi, now don't complain." He told her, before helping her to the front door. He knocked and her mother opened the door.

"Tempest, you had better have a good excuse." Her brown eyes blood shot, her brown hair tangled. She hadn't slept last night.

"Twisted ankle while hiking in the gorge, the park rangers found me." She admitted Jason nodded providing her with an alibi.

"I'm Jason." He smiled, "We found Tempest down in the gorge, if I may I'll help her inside." He said his voice sounding official. She nodded allowing him to help her into the house. Jason, to her embarrassment, went straight into Tempest's bedroom. She realized, to her horror, it was a mess of drawing and colouring supplies. There was a layer of laundry on the floor, and her dresser drawers were open. Her bed looked like a nest of blankets, books and writing supplies. Some things never changed. She may have been bored, but when she became bored, she became over active.

Jason laughed at her embarrassment, helping her to her bed. "I'll be back later." He then left, informing Tempest's mother that she had twisted her ankle. He assured her that Tempest would be fine in a few days. She heard the door close as he left the house.

Tempest's mother was to angry to talk to her, she heard her mother stomp downstairs. Tempest knew she was angry because she had been irresponsible, she had been raised better then that. Tempest didn't blame her, she knew she'd messed up. She dozed off until she heard pebbles hitting her window. Limping to her window, she opened it and removed the screen. Jason jumped in, landing silently on the floor. He looked at Tempest, then her ankle. "Sorry about that. You needed an excuse for not coming home." He held out her folder and hat. She took them, putting them in her backpack, hiding them from her family.

Tempest nodded "I know, but seriously, a twisted ankle. Couldn't you just say I just got lost?"

"Have you ever gotten lost before?" She shook her head, "then it's not believable. Look, Raven will heal you tomorrow morning. Right now, we need to set the portal." Tempest nodded, "okay, but first, why didn't time freeze when I left my world?" She was in this mess because time didn't freeze.

"Time moves differently, but can only ever march onwards." He watched her as he sat next to her on the bed.

"So if I think ten years?" She asked looking at the watch.

He shook his head, "don't wish away that time."

"If I think no time has passed?" She asked hopefully.

"Time always passes. The amount usually depends on you. That is why my world is sometimes called the timeless forest. Look," he sighed "I didn't ask you, you came of your own free will. No quest, magic didn't need you, you needed it. Magic wasn't coming apart at the seams so it had no need to freeze." She walked over and set the portal in a corner under an area rug. Jason nodded, "only one way to test it." She nodded and clicked the watch. Instantly, there was a flash of light and she was transported to her room in the magic tower. She clicked it again, and was back standing in front of Jason, in her own bedroom in the human world.

"COOL!" She laughed as he helped her to her bed, sitting down again. "I think I get it." She said softly "I'll be more careful with my time."

"Well, you better get some sleep. Raven's pretty serious when it comes to first year students. She means for you to get sleep and eat right. There are details in the papers Rhydian gave you." Jason told her. "I'll see you in a few days, after things calm down here. Don't use the portal until things calm down, see you." He leapt out the window, floating to the roof. She watched Greyhook take off soaring into the night. She laid down on her bed exhausted quickly falling asleep.

Morning came, and her mother walked in to check on her. She sat on the edge of Tempest's bed. "No more hiking until this room is clean!" She told her. Tempest nodded understanding. Her mother was only trying to protect her, even if it irritated her to be grounded. She waited until her parents had left for work before she tidied her room. Tempest had wrapped her ankle, which gave her enough support to move, if she was careful. It took her until almost noon to clean her room. The phone had rung half a dozen times that morning, her mother calling to check in on her. Tempest headed out to the kitchen, grabbing an apple, she went back to her room. She went through the paper work that Rhydian had given her, sitting down heavily at her desk.

The folder was a deep purple, like her hat, which sat on the corner of her desk. Inside the folder was a list of classes offered by the school. On the list of supplies, Rhydian had added a note saying he and Jason would gather her supplies. There was also a paper explaining what consisted of enough sleep, six to eight hours a night and food she had to eat, three good meals a day. It was apparently to make sure the first years had enough energy to survive the first of, hopefully, more years. There were also pamphlets on a summer camp. It looked like an ordinary camp, until she noticed a picture of Vlad, fixing a boat motor. Jason working with horses, and Raven waving at buses, all looking human. Camp councillors, Rhydian and Jason. Camp leader, Raven. Tempest shook her head, and flipped to the next pamphlet. It was a private school, again with Raven as the headmistress. Jason was listed as gym teacher and Rhydian was teaching technology. Vlad was listed as a history teacher. She could not help but laugh at these false pamphlets. At least she knew, if she wanted to go live at school, she had a way.

CHAPTER 8

VISITORS

S HE HEARD A COUGH BEHIND HER, Raven stood there. Tempest leapt to her feet. "Sorry I didn't hear you come in!" She said watching Raven as prey might watch a predator. Raven had been a warlord, and was a werewolf. Tempest winced, sitting heavily back down at her desk, "dumb ankle."

"Hello Tempest, I see you are going over the paper work, good. However, I would like to point out, that an apple does not consist of a meal." Raven told her smiling indulgently.

Tempest nodded, "don't worry, this is a snack. I'll make lunch soon." She tried not to seem nervous. It was not every day she had people drop into her room, though it seemed to be happening quiet a bit lately. Raven nodded, absently looking around. Tempest was suddenly glad she had cleaned her room. "When you see a class that interests you, circle it." Raven instructed, her sitting on the bed. "Now, let's see that twisted ankle." Tempest nodded, turning her desk chair to Raven. She held her ankle, unwrapping it. "I really must get Jason to volunteer at the clinic more, he does wonderful work." Her hands glowed. "There, all better Tempest. Just go easy on it." She let go of the foot. Tempest stood, slowly resting her weight on it. Raven nodded, walking to the teleport circle and was gone.

Tempest went back to the paper work, circling a couple of classes. Basic skills, species history and creatures 101. She also signed up for beginners flight training, which encompassed physical training. She figured it couldn't be worse then gym class.

"Hello Tempest!" She turned around seeing a red haired, freckled boy. His hair was sticking out at every angle. He wore jeans and a red T-shirt, no shoes though. "Rhydian, hi. How come you look so....normal?" She asked smiling at him.

He grinned showing sharp, pointed teeth. "Just a skill. I thought I'd drop in to say your supplies are all set. If you want, I can show you around tomorrow morning. You can change your mind any time, and live in our world. Jason said he'd take you to meet the one human living in our city, if you want."

Tempest nodded, "Yeah, ok. I'll come by tomorrow, by the way, is there anyway to put a door bell on that portal?"

He shook his head laughing. "Just think, what would happen if your family heard a door bell ding in here. Anyway, I'll see you tomorrow morning, bright and early." He walked back to the portal and vanished.

Tempest shook her head, going to the kitchen. She found rice crisps and scattered a few within the circle. She covered the circle back up, with the area rug. "Instant doorbell." She grinned sitting back at her desk. She went over the rules for school. There were only two rules listed in the rules section.

1)No Killing

2)Don't get caught breaking the guidelines.

The guidelines section was longer then the rules:

1) We recommend you don't fight outside of controlled environments.

2) Limited running in the halls if completely necessary it is allowed.

3) Return books to library on time.

4) Don't use unnecessary magic in the halls.

Tempest simply shook her head. Tomorrow was going to be interesting. She set her alarm for seven am, before stuffing the papers into her bag. She went back to the kitchen. She made a chicken caesar salad and started supper for her parents. They came home from their jobs. Her father, as usual, crashed on the couch watching TV with her brother Steve. He was twenty four and worked with her father in the electronics department of their fathers garage. His dark brown eyes watched her. He ran his hand through his brown hair. She thought for a moment that his eyes turned orange, but it must have been a trick of the light.

They enjoyed supper together. Her mother informed her that she was no longer grounded. That night, she could barely sleep. The clock ticked slowly down the hall. Each second felt like an hour. By the time dawn rolled around, she had just fallen asleep. She woke to the sounds of the coffee maker percolating. Her folks talking about money and school. They were two of the main worries around the house.

CHAPTER 9

SCHOOL EXPLORATION

T EMPEST ROLLED OUT OF BED, GETTING dressed in jeans and a t-shirt. She heard everyone leaving the house. Walking to the portal, standing in the circle, she clicked the watch. Instantly, she was transported through to her tower room. She walked to her door. Opening it, she let out a scream. Hanging upside down in the hall was Rhydian, playing with a piece of parachute cord. "Finally! Took you long enough to get here."

Tempest chuckled, "well I had to wait for everyone to leave, before vanishing." He dropped from the ceiling, landing on his feet. It was then, she realized, that the ceiling was covered in claw mark and places to hold on. "Many people travel by ceiling?" She asked. The ceiling was wooden, with studs acting as hand holds. There were others, carved in, by years of people traveling.

He nodded, "before my people retreated from Emor to their hidden cites, there were many here. We are builders after all."

She looked at him, surprised. "Why would your people leave this place? It looks amazing."

He lead her down a hallway, "this place became to loud for most of my people. The younger ones come here and study. The older people have gone home, most prefer our own hidden cities, where they live in peace and quiet."

"But not you?" He shook his head, leading her down to Raven's office.

"No I grew used to the noise. I do have my own sanctuary, besides, I am needed here. This place would fall apart without me." He knocked on Raven's door, and it swung open. Jason was there, with Vlad and Raven.

"I'm telling you, headmistress, we've looked everywhere. The only scent we've been able to find, is vampire. We have been unable to locate Scott." Jason slammed his hand on the table. The figures wobbled and some toppled.

She nodded looking at the boys, "alright, I'll ask the guards to assist. Perhaps he's just exploring his world, though, if you recall, you boys were untraceable. From time to time."

Jason nodded, "yes. But we had each other. Scott's barely eleven. We were in our young hundreds!" Jason then smashed fist onto the table a second time. "We could look after ourselves!"

Raven nodded, "I realize that, Jason. I must ask you two to calm down, I must speak with Tempest. If you two don't mind going to talk to Sarge. You can co-ordinate with the guard and perhaps locate Scott."

Jason nodded as he and Vlad left the room. Raven looked at Rhydian, "you may go as well. I will take care of Tempest today. See if you can locate Scott, and let me know when it will be approaching."

Rhydian nodded, "yes ma'am. I'll keep the tracker on." He then he left as well.

Raven stood leaning against the front of her desk. "What shall we see today?" She looked at Tempest. "We could go see the dwarves, or the fairy glades perhaps." She waited for Tempest to answer. Tempest grinned, asking "could you show me the AMS or this school?"

Raven nodded, "ok school tour it is." Raven chucked and lead her through the hallways. It was a pretty standard school. Classrooms, lockers and students. Occasionally, there was a student who flew through the halls, or used the ceiling. "This building is simply classrooms, and dorms. You've seen the large library well we have a smaller one here. Jason, will take you to the gym in a few days. You still must rest that ankle. We should be getting you home soon though. I believe your family will be home soon." She walked Tempest back to her room. "Listen, if you choose to study here, you will get the education of a lifetime. Go home and think." She left Tempest at her door, she entered her room and teleported home.

That afternoon, she laid down in her bed, just thinking. Of course she was going to join the school and learn to fly. She couldn't help wondering where Scott had vanished to. She read over some more of the paper work, waiting for her family to come home. When they did come home, she listened to them talk of their normal lives. It wasn't what she wanted, she realized. The normal work, daily 9-5 existence, no, she wanted adventure.

CHAPTER 10

ACCEPTANCE

S HE WANDERED OUT TO THE KITCHEN her mother started the dish water and it was like a bomb went off. The taps burst. Water shot everywhere, straight up, hitting the ceiling. Her father ran for the basement. Turning the water off for the house. Somehow Tempest knew this was her fault. She shook her head, starting to clean up the water. Her father came back with a mop and bucket. "That's all the taps in the house!" He shook his head. They started cleaning the kitchen, and then ordered pizza. Her parents left to talk to the insurance company and pick up new taps for the house, and pick up the pizza.

Tempest ran for the portal in her room, clicking the watch. She fell through, landing on the floor in the tower. Her decision to study magic, and the taps exploding couldn't be coincidence.

Jason ran through the door, followed by Raven. "What happened?" He came over to Tempest, gathering her in his arms. He placed her on the edge of the bed. Raven knelt in front of Tempest, staring into her eyes. "What happened Tempest?" She looked at Jason. "You said you stocked her room, towels please, Jason." He nodded, getting up and opening the top drawer. He pulled a couple towels and a blanket out and wrapped them around Tempest. He sat back down.

Tempest shook her head, "all the taps in the house exploded." She quietly stared at the floor.

Raven nodded, "I was afraid of this happening. You see, now that you've accepted magic and want to learn, magic is trying to claim your life."

Tempest looked at her in shock, "you speak of magic like it's alive." She nodded, "in a way, it is. Without magic, none of us would be here. It binds you to this world, it is the bridge between realms."

Tempest shook her head, "I accepted it was real, when I helped Jason."

Raven nodded, "yes, but you have chosen to follow magic. To come to our world, by your free will, not just for a quest. Think of it like rubbing socked feet on the carpet. The static builds and stays until it can discharge. The taps were the discharge." She explained watching her.

Tempest let out a sigh, "okay, so how do I avoid this happening again?" She dried her damp eyes on a corner of the blanket. She had been hysterical when she had teleported in.

Raven looked at Jason, who nodded. "We tire you out, both mentally and physically. We get you a magic prevention band. Also, I'll be going to your parents. To tell them you've been accepted, to a private military school." Raven watched the quiet girl in front of her. "Trust me, you'll be that tired, you'll need the excuse."

Tempest stared at her in astonishment. "You mean I'll have to live here. I don't want to live here!" She complained.

Raven shook her head, "we won't pull you from your home. We are pulling you from your school." She looked at Tempest, in the eye. She could see she'd already lost this argument. Raven nodded, "Jason will go get you something to eat, and I'll need to do some paper work. Get some rest." She left with Jason.

CHAPTER 11

MAGIC PREVENTION

T EMPEST SHOOK HER HEAD. IF THEY thought she was going to just sit still, after blowing up the taps at home, they had another thing coming. She went to her door, peeking out to see Jason, going down. She watched his rug disappear down the stairs before she slowly followed not bothering with the rug, she exited on Rhydian's floor. She walked through the supply room. Rhydian's room, the massive technological mess. She walked in, "hello, is anyone home?" Tempest called in, there was no reply. When she crossed the threshold, alarms blared. A red light turned on and a weighted net dropped onto her head "HELP!" She yelled, trying to claw her way out. The more she struggled, the tighter the net became.

"Tempest, what in the dragons guts are you doing here?" It was Rhydian, glaring at her from a hammock, high in the beams of the ceiling. He climbed down the nearest pillar, like a chameleon, head first. When he was about head height from the ground, he jumped down, landing on his clawed feet. "Magical disengage, authorization, Rhydian." The alarms stopped, and the net released her. She watched as it flew straight up, attaching itself to a set of hooks. She stood, brushing herself off. Rhydian stared at Tempest, waiting for an explanation. "Err hi, she said awkwardly.

"Hi," he responded, looking at her. "Now, what are you doing here?" He asked her.

She had the good sense to look embarrassed. "Umm, I err, Raven said I needed a magic prevention band. I thought you'd be the one to make it. Can I watch?"

He laughed, "I'm sure you can watch, since you'll be the one making it." He walked her to the table and bench. He cleared a space for her on the table, placing a box of thread in front of Tempest. "Pick a few colours." He instructed her. She nodded and sat at the table. She pulled out a blue, a green, a red and a yellow and handed them to Rhydian. Rhydian tied them around a nail in the table. He showed her how to braid them, before handing the threads over. "Go on, your turn." Tempest nodded and started braiding while he sat down and started talking. "Back a couple hundred years, Jason was turning three hundred. Emor was freshly built. Peace had just come to the land. Peace after a long bloody war between three races. My people, the werewolves and the vampires. There are still skirmishes to this day over land and food but it is more peaceful. There were others who participated as well but the main combatants were the three races." Tempest listened intently.

"Raven was the first to think about peace. To bring it to the table but she had lost the most of all the leaders. She convinced our elders, in each race, it would be a good will gesture to exchange children. The program lasted for fifteen years. Five years with each species, learning their customs and laws. We traveled as a group, spending time with each people, sleeping with knives under our pillows, one eye open. We traveled with a group from each of our clans but the three of us were kept together. The others made their own camps, but we were trapped with each other. When we reached a new people, there were celebrations and games that lasted for months. Jason and Vlad often tried to out preform each other, while I was happy to be left alone, with the books each species kept. We started enjoying or at least tolerating each others company. You see, our own kinds isolated us. We were pushed together, forced to get along. Turns out, we got along so well, we went to school together, learning here in Emor. Jason and Vlad competed during their time here at basic school. Chasing the same girls, playing the same sports, they were insane rivals. They eventually figured out they could get away with anything, because their species were known enemies. There was a good fifteen years of practical jokes and adventures then many followed as we started school here. Once they decided to specialize, we moved out to our own place. I am rarely there, but the others stay at the house when they are at school. Vlad went into magic, hard core. He's currently learning storm magic. Jason, on the other hand, went into animal magic."

Tempest tied off the end of the strings, "what about you? What are you studying?" She asked curiously.

He smiled, his tongue licking his lips. "Me, well I'm studying nothing, I am a creator and an inventor. The things I make are for both groups. I create to see what I can do. I believe in your world I would be called a scientist." He chuckled "to push the knowledge we have one step further and to look after newcomers. I also keep this place running in my spare time fixing anything that breaks." He unhooked the thread from the nail. He took her wrist, tying the threads. "That will prevent you from using magic in the human world. It's not the perfect solution. Eventually, your magic will surpass it. Hopefully, by then, you will have control. Now, you should go to your room. Jason will probably be there with food." Tempest headed out. As the door slid shut, she heard him yell, "and no more sneaking into my shop it's not a playground! Knock next time!"

CHAPTER 12

CLEAN UP

TEMPEST LEFT, HEADING TO THE STAIRS. "Twelfth floor please." She picked up a rug and placed it on the landing. She requested a floor and the rug whirled her up the stairs to her landing. She placed it back on the pile next to the landing going down the hall to her room. Jason had a couple sandwiches and two bowls of salad, sitting on the desk waiting for her.

"Here, eat first, get some grub in you. Then we can get you home. You have already visited Rhydian. I'll help you clear the water up." She sat down on her bed. Tempest took a sandwich and started eating chicken, lettuce and tomato sandwiches. They ate their meals, then they walked up to the portal. Jason went first, followed by Tempest.

She went, fetching towels from the hall cupboard. The mop and bucket were already waiting. They started cleaning up the water throughout the house. When they finished, Jason snapped his fingers. It wasn't until he did that did she realized time had barely passed. "Time bubble. I slowed time within this building so we could get the cleaning done."

Not five minutes passed and her parents arrived home. They came through the door, holding several bags from the local hardware store and a pipping hot pizza. "So your rescue ranger has come back Tempest?" She teased her daughter.

She blushed "MUM!" Tempest complained, as her father started replacing the taps. They started eating. Her father muttered about how the taps shouldn't have blown at all, let alone at one time.

"So Jason, why are you here?" She asked Jason. Tempest leaned back, watching him try to dig his way out of her mothers interrogation.

"I was actually returning Tempest's bike and noticed the mess. I offered to help clean up." He said smiling calmly.

"Well, that was very considerate Jason." They heard a rapping on the front door. Her mother stood, going to the door. "Yes, of course you may come in." She said to the person, as she walked back to the dinning room.

CHAPTER 13

NEW SCHOOL

RAVEN FOLLOWED HER MOTHER THOUGH TO the dinning room. Instead of her jeans and T-shirt, she wore a somber grey suit. Her hair was pulled back into a tight bun instead of purple. It was jet black like Jason's. She and Jason ignored each other, as she walked in. "Hello, my name is Raven. Please allow me to explain why I've come to call. I've come to offer Tempest, a fully paid scholarship, at our military school. The school starts at high school level and goes straight through to university. Our students often go on to the highest fields, it is the best education." Tempest stifled a laugh. 'Highest fields,' definitely. Unless another school was teaching cloud hopping. Raven shot Tempest a glare, setting her brief case on the table, showing Tempest's parents graphs and pamphlets.

"Well, this is quite impressive." Her mother admitted. "But where is this school. Would she be living there? How did you find Tempest? Why her?" She looked at Tempest, "it is her choice of course. She is old enough to make her own choices."

Raven nodded, "the school is located an hour from here. Most students are bused or drive. Usually, they live on campus. Coming home on weekends and holidays. The public schools keep record of their most brilliant. We review the lists and make our choices. A few are approached and accepted every year." Raven seemed so sure and confident, Tempest found herself believing the story. Raven looked over at her. "Tempest, your mother said it was your choice do you wish to come learn at our school?" Tempest nodded as Raven raised an eyebrow at her.

"Err, yes it would be a great opportunity. I'd love to mum. You are always saying you wish you could send me to university, this is my chance!" Tempest smiled, though she briefly wondered how this would show up on her transcript.

Tempest's mother nodded, "if you are sure Tempest. However, I need to know where you get the bus and when you will be home."

Raven nodded, "there is a bus that would pick her up." Raven pulled out a blank sheet of paper. Tempest's mother picked it up to read. She then got a pen and signed the bottom. "OK Tempest, you catch the bus tomorrow morning." Raven told her. "Be ready for a day. You will be back on the weekend."

Tempest nodded, "I should go figure out what to wear." She muttered trying to excuse herself.

Raven nodded "I will be going now to head back to the school and file her paper work." She got up, gathering her papers. She put them into her briefcase. "I'll send the bus for you in the morning, tomorrow is a Friday. It will be your orientation day."

Jason looked at Raven then Tempest. "I'm going to hang out a bit more. Tempest said she had quite a library and I wanted to take a look, if that's okay?" He asked looking at her mother who nodded.

"She has a few books, go on have fun." She had resigned to the fact that Tempest was going to be leaving home, for more time then she liked. Jason and Tempest took off for her bedroom, "leave the door open Tempest!" Her mother called after them.

"Yes, mum!" Tempest ducked into her room, Jason following. They heard Raven leave as the front door closed.

Tempest's mother cleaned up the kitchen. Jason was staring at the light as it flicked on. He pointed at it, tilting his head "electricity?" He asked, tentatively. Tempest nodded her head. "Yes, it's electricity" She smiled. She flicked it back off and he spun around, looking at Tempest. She turned the light back on. He turned to look at it like a startled cat. "I'd heard of it, but I've never seen it work." He admitted watching the light.

Tempest nodded, "go on then, you try it." She told him. He nodded, pressing the switch and leaping, as the light turned on and off.

"COOL!" He looked over at the books. The shelves filled the walls. Books more then filled the shelves, they were stuffed at random intervals. There were also several piles on top. He just looked at the books, "all fantasy?" Tempest shook her head, "half is history. Which I'm guessing, is missing parts where other species were involved."

He nodded, "not to worry. We will catch you up on the history. We will also work to wear you out. Obstacle course first. Tonight, after you say you are going to bed, come through and we will run you through the course. I'll introduce you to the only other human in Emor, when we have time." He smiled as he walked over, running a hand over the spines. He looked out the door, "I'll see you in an hour or two." He walked to the portal and leaping out of Tempest's world.

Tempest grinned, she got to start school tomorrow. A school she knew her family would disapprove of. It was also going to be far from boring. She was going to meet the only human living in Emor. The human was sure to have a unique perspective on the world. Tempest went to the front door, making a show of opening the door and saying good-bye to someone who had already left, before popping into the kitchen. "Mum I'm going to bed now."

She nodded, "yes okay, Tempest you have a big day tomorrow go to sleep. If you don't want to go, that's okay to." She meant the new school. Tempest had to admit she was feeling nervous.

"Mum, this is free university after I finish high school. I can't give an opportunity like that up." Tempest told her. Even though it was still before sunset, Tempest went to her room. She actually had no intention of sleeping, she just wanted an excuse to not be disturbed.

"OK dear go to sleep." Her mother said softly.

CHAPTER 14

OBSTACLES

TEMPEST CLOSED HER BEDROOM DOOR AND teleported through to the tower. Jason sat at her desk, waiting for her. "About time. Come on. We can get you running the obstacle course, and start wearing you down." He lead her outside and through the town. He took her out behind the flight school. It looked like a mad mans obstacle course. With thin boards, for running. It lacked safety ropes and nets. There were beams, rope ladders, floating platforms, tightropes and even swinging ropes.

Tempest looked at Jason in disbelief, "you except me to go up there?" She raised an eyebrow.

He nodded, an amused look on his face. "Go, on see that rope ladder, it will take you to the first level."

"What happens if I fall?" Tempest asked, watching the ropes sway in the wind. Even the platforms swayed in the breeze.

He chuckled, "there's a safety net of sorts, don't worry." He pushed her towards the ladder. She placed her hands on the bars and started the climb. Tempest was at least five feet off the ground on the first level. This level consisted of beams, going across to platforms. Above that level, were harder obstacles. The higher the course, the harder it became. Jason had said there was a safety net but Tempest didn't see one. She trusted him though, he climbed behind her. "Go on, it's okay." He gently pushed her across the beam and she traveled to the first platform.

Tempest was becoming far less sure that she wanted to keep moving. The breeze ruffled her hair, she looked down. Below her, on the ground, was a ground course with pits, tunnels and climbing walls. "Why couldn't we start down there!" Tempest complained, glancing over her shoulder at him. That was her first mistake. The wind hit Tempest in the chest, her arms pinwheeled. She fell sideways, her feet above her head. Tempest plummeted towards the ground, only to be stopped an arms length from where she had been. She dangled upside down, just below the beam. Jason stood above her, his arms crossed over his chest, a look of amusement across his face. "You gonna hang around all day, or do you want to try again?" He asked smiling.

"Pull me up!" She demanded staring at him.

He complied, grabbing her foot, pulling her up and onto the beam. "Being up here will improve your balance." He told her as they climbed down the ladder behind them. They reached the ground and jogged back to the tower. Instead of grabbing a rug to take them up, he had Tempest run the twelve flights up to her room. They reached her room and she activated the watch, going through the portal to her room in the human world.

Tempest went to her bed and fell asleep quickly. However when she woke in the middle of the night she was unable to sleep anymore. She got dressed in the dark. Going to the portal, she went through to her room in the tower. A dim light glowed in the ceiling of her dorm room. She looked around. On her desk was a class schedule, a black library robe, boots and clothes for the flight school. Next, she noticed the pile of books carefully shelved in the bookcase. She shook her head, pulling the flight clothes on. As she put the gear on, she noticed it shrunk to her size. The flight jacket even pulled her name into the stitching. She placed the helmet on. Her vision exploded. The visor allowed her to see the room, in perfect detail, even though it was only dimly lit by the glowing light in the ceiling. She pulled the gloves on. They were leather and went into the jacket cuffs. She looked at the window, lifting the visor. Her reflection looked back at her, she looked amazing.

CHAPTER 15

FIRST DAY OF CLASS

TEMPEST SNAPPED THE VISOR DOWN. LOOKING out the window, through the visor, she could see Emor laid out before her. To her right was the Nest and on her left was the AMS, Advanced Magic School. Laid out between the towers, was the city. Winding roads lit by their magic lights. Farther, past the city limits, trees, a forest of trees. Far in the distance, to the west, there were the shimmering lights from the mortal world. To the right, the mountains. It was odd seeing humanity encroaching on the magical world. Her own world, so far away in some ways, but so close in others.

Tempest turned from the window, opening her door. She snuck up the stairs and climbed to the top of the tower. She went out the trap door, to the outside tower. Battlements surrounded the edges. Tempest walked to the edge, looking over and down. She had lost count of the number of floors she had climbed past. What she saw below, were the planets rotating around the tower.

The whole world seemed to be holding it's breath. She took the helmet off and set it on the wall. Tempest stared out into the darkness, the air felt electrically charged. Lighting raced through the clouds around the AMS. She looked up. High above her were the stars, burning brighter than she had ever seen them. Tempest sat on the wall, her feet dangling above the planet Saturn, as it slowly rotated. Then, it happened. The sun came over the horizon, the whole world started to breath. From the birds, starting to sing, to the people far below, starting to leave their homes. From up where she sat, they appeared to be ants. Tempest saw huge bats, flying to the flight school. They roosted within the tree structure as a flock of dragons and gryphons flew out. She picked up her helmet and turned back around, to go back to her room. When she placed her feet on the stone of the tower, she felt it hum to life. Tempest went to the stairwell. The stairs were flooding with rugs coming off all the floors, she jogged down not wanting to be late. She took the stairs, two at a time. When she reached her floor, she leapt off to find her schedule posted on her door. Friday's class was labeled flight school. She pulled the schedule down. Folding it up, she put it in her pocket and took off running for the Nest.

She knew she was late. She had gotten lost on her way through the city. Finally, she ran into the tree school. She saw a line of nine other students, standing in front of a man he looked, in every sense of the word, a drill sergeant. Right down to his buzz cut, square head. She looked at him carefully and she noticed his yellow eyes and rounded ears. "So nice of you to join us Cadet Tempest, file in!" He spoke much louder then he necessary. Tempest went to the end of the line. "I don't like girls, especially not weak human girls!" He yelled standing in her face. "So Cadets because of this humans lack of respect for you and this class, you get to clean the Dragon's Den this morning!" He roared, "now move it, and take this human with you!" The other cadets took off running for a tunnel leading underground, she followed them quickly.

One of the cadets turned and lifted her visor. Her face was covered in tiger stripes, her eyes a vibrant reflective yellow. "Don't worry about the commander, his name is Sarge, he always picks on the new person. Whether they are male or female, it's his training method." She grinned, "there are people who hate humans. He doesn't, he's hard on everyone so I wouldn't worry. I was last weeks pick." She chuckled, jogging ahead of Tempest. She followed quickly. They reached a cave mouth, located beneath the tree tower. "I'd put your helmet on, if I were you. That is, if you don't want to trip over your own feet. The dragons don't like bright lights, they are comfortable in low lights. When they go outside, a second eyelid covers their eyes, to protect them." She explained to Tempest. "By the way, I'm Laura. This is where the dragons, who aren't bonded to permanent riders, reside. We clean their caves, feed them and scrub their scales. I'll show you the ropes. Sometimes it's the Gryphons Eyrie we clean, but we never do the Bat Branches. Only certified riders can do those. Bats are temperamental." She snapped her visor into place. Tempest did the same as she walked into the cave. It wasn't dank or even truly dark. It was lit by low glowing moss, it was warm and inviting.

The caves were set as a stable for dragons. Beside each door, a shovel rested. On each door, was a name plate. Laura showed her how to clean the rooms and fill the food dishes. The food was harvested from the glowing moss. The dragons waited patiently, outside their stalls, when it was time to wash their scales and stalls. It didn't take long, working as a team. They finished within the hour. They headed back to the commander, who stood waiting for them. "Get out and run laps around the obstacle course." He ordered, as they arrived in front of him. The cadets spent the rest of the day running around a track, around the ground obstacle course. After that, it was back off to the magic school, for Tempest to teleport home for the weekend.

When she arrived home, she caught left overs in the kitchen. As everyone came in they went about their regular activities which in this case was watching TV in the living room. The next morning she rolled out of bed, her muscles were achy. She stumbled, hitting the ground. Her mother walked into the room, grinning. "Tired Tempest?" She only grunted and nodded. Tempest spent the weekend hanging out with her family. She itched for Monday, when she would be going to her first magic class. The weekend went slowly, but eventually, it ended on Sunday night, just as it always did.

CHAPTER 16

ACCIDENTS HAPPEN

MONDAY MORNING CAME AND TEMPEST HEARD her mother moving in the kitchen. "Tempest, breakfast is on the table, I have to go to work!" She called back to her.

Her brother, Steve, was already up at the kitchen table. "Hey Tempest, how was school?" He asked as she came into the kitchen.

She shook her head, sitting heavily at the kitchen table in front of her bowl of cereal. "Gym is gonna kill me." She smiled as he pushed his glasses further up his nose. They were just like her fathers, aviator geek glasses. "You know, there is no shame in not being the best." He looked up from his book on microchips. It was leaning against the orange juice. As it started to slid, he took and closed it. "Look at me I'm stuck reading up on these microchips in the cars because when our father looks at computers they crash."

"I'll have you know, I'm far from the best at this school, Steve. I just don't want to lose my scholarship." She admitted, as he placed the book on the table, pouring them both orange juice.

He nodded, "I know kid, just take it slow." He got up, putting his dishes on the counter. Once her brother had left for work, and she had finished eating, she went back to her room.

She teleported to her dorm room. Putting her hat on, as she headed down to the first floor. Her next day of class was to take place. Basic skills. Vlad stood at the front of the room, in a class that consisted of people of all species ages five to ten. Tempest sat down heavily at a desk that was to small for her. The kids stared at her, the human. "Good, now that we are all here, I'd like to introduce Tempest, the human. Now down to today's class. Can anyone tell me the elements?" Most of the students started bouncing in their chairs, eager to answer.

"Earth, Fire, Water and Wind!" Said one kid when Vlad pointed to her.

Vlad nodded, "and why do we not turn ourselves into the elements? Why do we simply ask them to work with us?"

Another one of the kids answered, "we can lose ourselves as the elementals did."

Vlad nodded, "good. Now, who wants to tell the story of the elementals?" He watched the class. No one spoke, no one moved. It was like they were all waiting for him, to tell a story. Vlad sat on the edge of his desk. The lights dimmed, he started to speak. "Long before the great war, when humans only occupied a small island, there were four races. The Flames, the Wets, the Stones and the Winds. These people were so connected to the elements, legend has it, anywhere there was fire, a Flame could walk. Anywhere a puddle, a Wet could appear. Stones could jump out of the very earth and the Winds could create breezes to travel on. As time went on, they lost themselves to the very elements they thought they controlled. That is why, until you go to AMS, you will not be taught to control elements. You are taught to ask them for help even after attending the AMS asking the elements for help over trying to control them is preferred. They lost themselves to the elements. Now, you will start class by asking water to fill the glasses." He told the class, handing out plastic cups.

Tempest took hers and looked around, watching the kids stare silently at the cups. Tempest thought about the problem then nodded. "Air, please release the water you hold." The next thing she knew, they were all soaked to the bone. The cups were full, and Vlad was staring at Tempest. She saw Vlad rushing towards her, as she collapsed, falling out of her chair towards the ground. Vlad caught her, holding Tempest to his chest. Vlad muttered, "stupid human," as darkness claimed her.

When Tempest woke, she was in her room in the tower. It was dark out, though Raven sat at her desk. "Um, hi," Tempest managed as she tried to sit up. Raven was there in a moment. A hand on her chest, holding her down. "Don't, I don't want you vomiting again." She growled quietly. "Tempest you must be more carful. Tomorrow, you will report to my office. We will speak of your classes, and your detention. Go to the flight training, then my office.

No sneaking to the top of the tower." With that, she walked out the door, vanishing into darkness.

Jason shot through the door after she left. "Your lucky to be alive Tempest! If Vlad hadn't been there, you would be dead!" He picked up a bottle of water and helped her drink. He sat down on the edge of her bed. "Your lucky Raven didn't lock your magic, she could do that." Fear was in his voice. "She did it to me, once. Go to sleep now. I just wanted to make sure you were alright." She only nodded. Having drunk her fill, she was happy to rest. She closed her eyes, falling back to sleep within moments.

CHAPTER 17

GRYPHON

WHEN TEMPEST WOKE UP, SHE PUT on her flight suit, then headed out the door. Laura stood, waiting for her at the staircase. "Come on, I'm your escort for the morning. We are to go clean first, and it's your first flight class today." She nodded, following her down the stairs. They left the tower, going through the town. They went into the Nest, straight down to the Dragons Den, to clean. Tempest felt happy to be busy.

They had cleaned a couple stalls, when the commander marched in, announcing, "Tempest, Laura, Jason is waiting for you two in the roosts, get moving." Laura nodded, before leading Tempest up. She tied a rope around their waists, climbing the tree tower interior. They went all the way to the top, climbing one of the main ladders. As they reached the top of the ladder, Tempest realized there were no platforms, just beams. They looked as though they could break under a feathers weight. Jason stood on a beam that tilted up into the canopy. Laura went up first, showing her how to place her feet, safely. She climbed on her hands and knees holding on tightly to the edges. When they reached the upper canopy, Jason lead them to where three gryphons were waiting for them. Jason's Greyhook, and two much smaller ones, only the size of small ponies. Each had a saddle kit next to it. "These are the training mounts, miniature gryphons. Gryphon riding is the easiest to learn. Dragons are more difficult, as they can fly upside down and are able to surpass the sound barrier. They can fly to the highest parts of the atmosphere, also, the scales make them slippery." Jason smiled, "this is the whistle to call a gryphon." He whistled, "anywhere you are, it will call a gryphon. Usually, the one you've been paired with."

"What about the bats?" Tempest asked. She looked curiously around herself, hunting for the elusive creatures.

Jason shook his head, "I start my bat training next week. You must be one with them to fly, complete trust. I have worked the past few years earning that trust. They can fly high enough to leave the atmosphere, for short periods of time. Their fur can hold oxygen, to allow breathing. There are also the Rays. Giant manta rays, who fly both above and below water. Later this year, we will be taking a group to the oceans, to learn about them." Greyhook nipped his shoulder. "Today, though, we will fly the noblest, most jealous of creatures." Greyhook nipped his shoulder, again. "OK," he said. He began showing them how the saddles went on. The buckles and straps, to prevent them from sliding off.

Once they were strapped in, and ready to go, he leapt onto Greyhook's saddle. Greyhook jumped over the edge, their own gryphons followed, leaping off, diving towards the ground. Halfway down the tree, the gryphons spread their wings and pulled up. They flew over the town, high enough that they wouldn't hit any of the houses. Jason lead them around the towers. The beat of the wings, the speed, it was astounding. The adrenaline rush was amazing. The ground spread beneath them. Jason lead them back to the tower, landing in the canopy.

Landing was, by far, the worst. They slowed down, but it was a sudden stop. Jason came over, helping the girls down. Tempest fell off, as the last strap came undone. He chuckled, helping her up. "Gotta get your land legs back. Anyway, you guys get to clean these two up. I'll refill the water." He walked to the water trough. He used a pulley to bring a bucket from the well, next to the trough. "When once you have tasted flight, you will forever walk the earth with your eyes turned skyward. There you have been, and there you will always long to return." Tempest smiled and shook her head he was probably right. She looked at the well, a well on a tree top tower. Would anything surprise her anymore?

Jason taught them how to groom the gryphons. They had to use two different brushes, a wire one, for the fur and a soft brush for the feathers. It took half an hour. Then they had to clean the tack, oiling the leather. As they finished, two more students came up. Jason dismissed the girls. Laura lead Tempest down the tower and through the town, taking her back to the magic tower. Laura dropped her off at Raven's office.

"Thank you Laura." Raven said she was sitting at her desk. Laura nodded, turning, she left Tempest, standing in front of Raven. She didn't even look up, making her stand there, shifting slightly from foot to foot.

CHAPTER 18

TARRED AND FEATHERED

RAVEN LET TEMPEST STAND THERE FOR five minutes, before she looked up. "Tempest, your detention is to be taken from the starter classes. Vlad will be teaching you here, and at the AMS. Your schedule will be changed. Now, get to the small library here, Vlad will meet you there. The rest of your time will be spent in the Nest." Raven told her, before waving her hand. Tempest was dismissed. She groaned. Having to spend more time running the obstacle course, was not her idea of fun. "Now, move it Tempest!" She called, after her sending her on the way. Tempest had been dragging her feet, down the hall. She sped up, walking faster down the hall, turning into the room that held the small library.

Rhydian stood in front of a bookcase, messing with a string of copper. "Okay Tempest, I've been assigned as your history teacher." He turned to her. He handed Tempest a book titled, 'The Great War,' "a thousand page essay. You have two weeks." He told her, grinning. "Raven did tell me to keep you busy, until Vlad picks you up. Vlad will take you to magic class everyday that you are not running at the Nest."

Tempest looked at him, "Rhydian what did I do wrong? I haven't been aloud to go anywhere on my own all day!"

Vlad walked in, "you, Tempest shouldn't have been able to get the air to release all of it's water at once. The air complied, to easily, for someone of your skill level. You've got everyone on edge, including Raven. I haven't seen her so irritated in years. Last time she was like this, Jason had used a human card trick on her." Rhydian head shook with laughter. "Now, that was one of the greatest jokes ever!"

"So let me get this straight. I'm in trouble because I completed the task I was given?" She was feeling angry and resentful. Vlad nodded, then shook his head, exasperated. "You're not really in trouble, so much as, Raven wants to keep an eye on you. You have to learn to control your magic."

"Still sucks." Tempest said pouting. Ice cold water poured over her head, "what was that for?" She spluttered, wiping water from her eyes. She shook her hair, trying to get the water out of her face. Vlad raised an eyebrow, "for acting like a spoiled brat. Now first lesson, don't ask for anything open ended. For instance, I asked the air to release a bit of cold water on your head. Unlike yesterday, when you flooded the class room. With your request for it to release all it's water." He chuckled as she felt the water run off her, leaving her dry.

"Right, and I shouldn't have been able to do that because I'm new."

Vlad nodded, "so we are going to work on your control, before you get yourself killed. Ask for something big and that can happen. A spell can drain your very being, your spirit." He told her, before setting a couple feathers on a desk, "here sit." She sat, slowly, on the chair. Staring at the feathers as though they were going to bite her. "Ask the air to lift that feather." He pointed at one of the feathers. It was speckled black and white, sitting in the middle of the pile.

Tempest stared at it, then quietly requested, "air, please lift the feather." All the feathers flew up to the ceiling, sticking there. Vlad sighed, shaking his head. "You had better get them off the ceiling." He exchanged a look with Rhydian, they were both doing their best not to laugh.

"Air, please let the feathers go." The feathers drifted down from the ceiling, going in every direction, just drifting hither and thither. Vlad shook his head, "pick them up." She moved to get up, but he placed his hands on her shoulders. "Use magic," he instructed. Tempest sighed, one of the feathers skirted off target. It had been the only one, that was going to land on the desk. Her frustration had caused it to just miss the desk. "Come here you rotten little feathers," she grumbled. "Air, bring me the feathers." Before she had time to blink, all the feathers were stuck to her, as though she had just been tarred and feathered, which in a way, she had been. Rhydian and Vlad howled with laughter. Rhydian was doubled over with mirth, while Tempest sat covered in feathers. She sighed, trying to physically remove them, only to find them stuck fast to her. When Rhydian could once again catch his breath, he stood, still trying not to laugh. He walked around Tempest, admiring her magnetic personality. Vlad placed his hands on her shoulders. "Tempest close your eyes and relax." He told her, gently rubbing her shoulders. The tension melted away and she felt the feathers melt away, trickling to the ground. She felt extremely tired and looked up at Vlad, who shook his head. "Tempest, come on, we'll go to the cafeteria and get you something to eat. You didn't eat a proper breakfast this morning did you?" Vlad asked. Tempest she simply shook her head. She was to tired to argue about what constituted of a proper breakfast. She had, in fact, skipped her breakfast.

Vlad looked at Rhydian, who nodded, "I'll help carry her. At this rate, she's going to need a lot of help." They each took one of her arms, helping her up. Vlad looked across her back, "you volunteering to help her all day?"

"No, Vlad. Just stating the obvious. I'm sure Jason would love a progress report. He's probably up in my tech room, catching some sleep. He's working with the bats tonight." Vlad nodded, "you couldn't pay me enough to fly on those demons, no offence Vlad."

CHAPTER 19

LUNCH TIME

THE GUYS HELPED HER OUT OF the library and down the hall. The smell of food wafted from the cafeteria as they walked in. She noticed the walls were covered in murals, showing different places and species, like all the murals around Emor. The floor was a tiled pattern. This was an amazing room, displaying many of the sights in the magic world. There were round tables, everywhere, with chairs surrounding them. In the centre of the room, was a large rectangular table, covered in all types of food. The far end was covered in desserts and an ice cream bar. At the near end were meats, fruits and vegetables. There were very few grains and breads. The boys deposited her at an empty table. She placed her head on her arms and closed her eyes. Within a few seconds, she was asleep. Tempest woke with a start, when Vlad placed a plate piled with vegetables and a glass of fruit juice in front of her. It was only noon, but she felt as though she would sleep for a week. She started eating, slowly at first, then dug in. Tempest hadn't realized she was starving. She was starting to see Raven's point, about eating decent meals and getting enough sleep.

Vlad and Rhydian collected their own food. As they sat, some of their friends came by, talking over her head to other people. Tempest realized, for the first time, she may be one of the only humans here, but she was not the centre of the galaxy.

"Guys, I know I'm sort of grounded, but you can go back to your friends. I'm just going back to the flight school after I eat. I'll be fine, I'll behave, no magic I promise." Tempest said holding her hand over her heart.

Vlad raised an eyebrow, "if you're sure Tempest. If you can find your way to the school, I've got studies. I'm sure Rhydian has an experiment running. Jason will pick you up later, to take you to the human. Her name is Rain." Vlad informed her. He looked at her very sternly, "no magic right?" She simply nodded to tired to answer.

"See you later Tempest, stay out of trouble." Rhydian ruffled her hair gently. Vlad nodded as they finished eating, before heading off to their own lives.

Tempest grinned at the prospect of freedom. Not that it mattered, she didn't plan on getting into any trouble. She gathered a few more vegetables, then she went to the dessert end, walking around it. She picked up a couple of cookies and a milkshake. She went back to her table, sitting and eating, admiring the walls. The mural on the wall in front of her was that of a jungle. It looked far more alive than any other picture she'd seen of a jungle. The colours were more vibrant then she'd ever seen. The murals must have helped the homesickness, giving the students pictures of home to look at. She stood as she finished eating. Turning around, she walked down the hallway, outside towards the flight tree. Once there, she went down to the Dragons Den, getting to work, washing scales and cleaning. There was another set of students working. They chattered amongst themselves, leaving her to her own devices.

CHAPTER 20

ASSIGNMENTS

S HE COULD NOT WAIT TO GET back in the air. She was so engrossed, in washing the scales on one dragon, that she failed to notice Sarge walk in. "Tempest, your name has been added to the squadron lists. In an hour, you will go read the board, then report to the main room. The board, is on the wall, next to the entrance." He left her to continue cleaning. When Tempest finished asking the the dragon to return to it's stall, she went to the main room. She found the list, attached to the board. She skimmed it, until she came to her name. She was under squad nine: Squad Leader-Tempest, Navigator/supply clerk-Laura, Medic-Rebel.

Tempest grinned. It wasn't the alpha teams, which were one through five. They were barely Beta at nine. They weren't Epsilon or Zeta, which were the bottom two teams. She looked to the centre of the room. The five teams of Beta, were gathering in front of the commander. Each team consisted of three people. Laura stood next to a boy, about four feet tall with rounded cat ears and sharp yellow eyes. He was thin and lithe. He looked around at Tempest. His ears swivelled towards her, on the top of his head. He said nothing, but elbowed Laura, who waved her over. She jogged over, standing at attention, as the hour came to a close.

The commander walked over to stand before them. "Your squadrons have been chosen. You will all start as trainees. Once you become riders, you can choose which creature you wish to specialize with. After that, if you are good enough, you'll be asked to join the guard." He told them, "now, out to the

obstacle course. You have an hours run, then you are dismissed for the day."
He watched as they jogged out to go run the ground course.

Tempest jogged with Laura and Rebel, "Hi I'm Tempest." They started
the course. The first obstacle they came to was a rock wall.

"I'm Rebel, Laura said your cool." He glanced at Laura, "you wanna do it
or shall I?"

"Thanks, didn't know I was cool, but thanks." Laura waved for him to go
first. He crouched down, then leapt vertically. He gripped the wall and held
out a hand to help her up. Laura leaped past Tempest, already at the top of
the wall, straddling it.

Tempest shook her head, starting to climb. Rebel nodded, "Sarge said
you were a stubborn one." He chuckled. She nodded, she knew she was stubborn. She was not going to let being human slow her down. She had to
prove herself to them, if she was going to lead the team. She climbed the
wall, reaching the top, her arms shaking. Rebel gently pulled Tempest up by
the scruff of her uniform. They ran through the course, a mud pit to swing
over, a fence to climb under, a pool to swim through. As they completed the
course, they were among the last to leave, but no one seemed to mind. "You
guys want to grab supper?" Rebel asked. "I know a decent pizza place nearby.
We have to wash first, but we can go there if you wish."

Laura nodded, "sure, come on Tempest. You can get to know us a bit
better, seeing as were going to have to depend on each other. We're a team,
even if it's just a starter team. Many starter teams stay together, just look at
Vlad, Rhydian and Jason."

"I'd love to, but I'm on detention." Tempest was embarrassed that she was
unofficially grounded.

Rebel chuckled, "you're only in trouble, if you get caught. We won't let
Raven catch you. You can rely on us, we're your squad." Laura nodded,
agreeing with Rebel. They headed in to the showers, girls were on one side of
a wall, guys on the other. They quickly washed the mud and sweat off themselves, before throwing their laundry into a basket. Laura tossed her a clean
pair of pants and a tank top. When they emerged, Rebel was waiting for
them, leaning against the wall. He grinned, seeing the girls, "you guys clean
up nice!" He said jokingly, as they headed out to the streets. They followed
Rebel through the city to the pizza place.

CHAPTER 21

BUSTED

THEY FOUND A TABLE AND REBEL went and ordered the pizza. When he arrived back at the table, Tempest looked at him. "So, where are you guys from?" Tempest asked "not that I know where anything really is here without my map card." She added quickly.

Rebel grinned and sat down. "My people are from the deep jungle, like Laura's. Both our ancestors were cats." The pizza was placed before them. It was the largest pizza Tempest had ever seen. The pan was at least three large pizzas worth. "You couldn't ask for better team mates." His sharp teeth showed when he smiled. "We, as a species, may have short attention spans, but we are loyal and observant."

Tempest looked at Laura. "So, if she's a tiger, what are you?" She asked, as they dove into the pizza. Each taking a slice and talking between mouthfuls.

Rebel's tail wrapped around his waist as he ate. His tail acted as a belt. It appeared to be, how they stopped people from treading on their tails. "Fossa, he's a fossa." Laura said as his mouth was full.

"Human world, what's it like?" Rebel asked watching Tempest. "The commander doesn't let us over the boarder and the patrols stop us if we try unauthorized. It's drilled into us to avoid the mortal world and humans, unless absolutely necessary."

Tempest smiled swallowing her mouthful of pizza. "Well, we have electricity, family and food. You guys should come visit. Sell it to my folks that I'm going to school. A regular, run of the mill school...." She glanced at their ears, "can you guys look a bit more human, like Jason and the others?" She asked curiously.

Laura nodded, "yes, of corse we can. It's only an illusion. It'd be cool. Not many magic people get to go to the human realm. As Rebel pointed out, we don't travel to the human world." She ate another slice.

Between the three of them, they had half the pizza eaten. The pair showed no sign of slowing. Tempest was almost done. "We'd have to go through Sarge, or Raven. If we sneak off, the detention you've got now, would look like a vacation."

"What about you guys, what are your homes like?" Tempest asked softly. She was on her last slice.

Rebel smiled, "in the deep jungle, the shadows can eat you. The spiders, the size of a pin head, can kill you in a moment with venom. Their webs, however. can be large enough to catch a person. So basically, anything and everything can kill you. We learn fast how to protect ourselves."

"I'm not from the deep jungles, I'm from the outskirts," Laura admitted grinning. "Not nearly as dangerous."

"I grew up in a tree top village. If you climb to the top of all the layers, you can see an ocean of green. From the time I was born, my feet had never touched solid ground. Where I grew up, my father was the defence commander, in the jungle. That was before Raven asked him to come work here." Rebel smiled, "just came of age last year, so the commander decided it was time I came with him, to Emor to learn."

Tempest heard a cough behind her. "Cadet Tempest, I believe you were supposed to report to the tower, after class." She heard Jason's voice as she turned to him. He stood with his arms crossed over his chest, that stupid smirk on his face, and his eyebrow raised. His green eyes staring into hers.

"Hi Jason I'd like you to meet my squad, Laura and Rebel." She'd failed to realize, they had both jumped to their feet. Jason was a higher rank then any of them, a teacher. She felt Rebels foot kick her chair leg. Jason's eyes shot to Rebel. If looks could kill, Rebel would have dropped dead. Tempest jumped to her feet, "Sorry sir I was-" Rebel kicked her, she shut her mouth,

standing at attention.

"Wait for me outside, Cadet Tempest. We have a trip to pay to the only other human in Emor." Tempest nodded scurrying out to the street. Jason followed a few minutes later. He lead her down the street, past a multitude of stores, cafes and people. Dusk was slowly approaching, as they walked up to a small wartime cottage. Jason lead her up the path, to the front door. He used the old lion head knocker.

CHAPTER 22

RAIN

"I'M COMING, I'M COMING." CAME A female voice. As the door was pulled open, Tempest saw the last sight she was expecting. Before her, stood a women in her thirties. She could have been her older sister. Blond hair cascaded around her shoulders, blue grey eyes with a shot of green stared back at her. Her nose was sharper and her skin was weathered. She smiled and held her arms open in greeting. "Hello little one." She embraced Tempest. Even her voice had a ring of familiarity to it. "Come in, come in. Raven said you would be dropping by. I made fudge and cookies." She lead them into a sitting room. There was an old dog lying on a blanket on the couch. His tail wagged as he saw Jason and Tempest. Looking around, she saw pictures of her family, going back over three hundred and fifty years.

On the table sat cookies and fudge. Tempest picked up the fudge, nibbling the corner, her eyes shot open in shock. "That's my grandfathers recipe!" She said shaking her head. The woman nodded, and pointed at a baby picture with Tempest's real name Rain and nickname Tempest under it.

The woman smiled, "yes, it's handed down the family line. From my mother, to me and to my children." She told Tempest "I'm your-"

Tempest cut her off, "you're a bunch of greats grandmother Rain." She jumped to her feet. She hugged her, "you're the woman I'm named after!" Tempest was so excited. "You went missing over three centuries ago, just vanished, into thin air!"

She nodded, "yes, Raven asked me to help, just as Jason asked you. I was asked to help Raven bring peace and then I helped to build this place. Now, sit. I want you to tell me all about your family and brother!" She grinned as they sat back on the couch.

Tempest nodded, and started telling Rain of her parents, and her older brother Steve. She in turn told Tempest of the relatives who'd died, before she was born, and about herself. She'd graduated from AMS and was a part time teacher. She was also the bat instructor. They talked until they reached the subject of Tempest's magic. By now, it was very late and only growing later, close to midnight. Rain had had a similar problem, with her magic being to powerful. She told Tempest of a few tricks to keep control.

Finally, Tempest asked the one question she dreaded the answer to most. "Why did you choose to stay here?"

Rain looked at her, as though measuring her, trying to figure out how much of the truth to give. "I chose to stay because, I fell for the buildings, this place, the peoples, the society, I fell in love." Rain sat watching Tempest, waiting for her to respond. Tempest nodded, slowly trying to understand how Rain could leave her family. "You see Tempest, I couldn't go back. This place stole my heart. It became a part of me. I did keep watch on the family, in case they needed me. And I have visited a few times. The human world was no longer for me," she admitted. "Now, Jason did mention you have a gift with animals. Nurture it. There are some conversations words cannot convey. I believe I should let you go to the tower dorms now, but feel free to visit, whenever you wish." She told Tempest. As they left, Rain hugged them, "guard your heart. This place can consume you." She waved them goodbye.

Jason took Tempest back to her room in the tower. She dropped onto her bed, as he sat down across the room at the desk watching Tempest. He tossed a large snails shell "tell it a number, it'll call a phone in the human realm. Tell your mum you had a good first official day, and goodnight." She nodded, doing as she was instructed.

Tempest called her house and left a message on the answering machine. "I don't even want to know how or why that works, do I?"

He shook his head chuckling, "probably not. It's one of Rhydian's inventions. Look Tempest, your grandmother's right. This place can consume you. In her defence, she did keep an eye on your family." Tempest nodded, slowly, "how come she hasn't aged?" He stared out the window, watching Pluto as it passed her window.

"Magic slows the aging process." He said softly, "by the time she was ready to go back, ten years had passed out in the mortal world. Her family had moved on. It didn't make sense for her to try to go back. She is one of the founders. Raven, Vlad's father and one of Rhydian's cousin's, all helped forge the peace we live with. Her sacrifice, helped my world a great deal."

Tempest nodded, "tell me about growing up here?" She asked as she brought her feet up and lay back on her bed.

Jason shook his head, "another night Tempest. For now you need sleep." He got up and moved towards the door. "There are pyjamas in the dresser." Tempest got changed into shorts and a tank top as the light above her dimmed.

CHAPTER 23

ADVANCED MAGIC SCHOOL

WEDNESDAY DAWNED, AS SHE ROLLED OUT of her bed. She put on a heavy cloak, over jeans and a t-shirt. She also put on a pair of rubber soled sneakers. Today, she was going to the AMS with Vlad. He stood, talking with Raven, at the bottom of the staircase. She approached them, hearing her ask Vlad, "still no sign?"

Vlad shook his head "no ma'am, Jason's down with the dwarves now, searching the caves." Raven sighed, "the boy has got to be around here. Have you tried the fairy glades?"

He shook his head, "no luck tried there yesterday," she nodded worriedly. "Come along Tempest." He called to her. Tempest emerged from the bottom of the stairs, looking sheepish.

She followed Vlad, as he lead her through the city, to a tall stone tower. Halfway up the tower was encompassed in clouds. Lightning danced within the clouds, thunder rattled the air around them. He walked through an open arch, leading into the tower. The Advanced Magic School tower felt darker, more dangerous. Even the air seemed serious and heavy. Vlad lead her down the hallway, as fog rolled around their ankles. He took her into a classroom, leaving her in the centre of the room. "Stay," he ordered, walking to one side of the room. He clapped his hands, the floor came to life. Flames danced through the mortar in the floor. "Keep the fire away from you." He ordered, his voice as hard and cold as steel.

She flinched, feeling the heat. She backed away, only to realize the flames were behind her as well. "Why are you doing this?" She called to Vlad, he didn't answer. Instead, a stake of fire shot towards her. Vlad wielded it expertly, causing it to dance around her. "Stop it!" She yelled, panic seeping into her voice. The fire died out completely.

"AGAIN!" He ordered. The room lit up, again flames danced around her. Panic swelled in her chest again.

The door swung open, instantly she was drenched in water. The flames died out again. "What is going on here?!" Came her grandmothers voice. "Vladamire what have I said? This is not how we treat---" She stopped, looking at Tempest. "Vladamire you've got exactly two minutes to tell me what you think your doing to my granddaughter."

Vlad looked her in the eye, as he walked forwards "Raven appointed me to train her, to teach her to control her magic."

She nodded, "Vladamire leave." Her voice deadly serious. He nodded, leaving the room. Rain spun towards Tempest, flames flew from her hands, lashing out towards Tempest. "Use your head, don't panic and above all stay calm!"

"Oi, I'm not a barbecue!" Tempest yelled, ducking more flames as they danced towards her.

"Would you prefer I let Vlad teach you?" Rain called across the room to her. "He would hold no reservations to burning you to a crisp."

"No ma'am." She said, grinning. somehow this felt better somewhat safer. They stopped for a lunch break, which was soup and crackers. It was a reminder, that she needed to eat more often, while in this school. They continued on after lunch. Flames shooting Tempest, burning her. By the end of the day, she was deflecting the flames, most of the time. She suffered several burns, but she was feeling more confident with her magic. Rain walked her back to the tower that night. Tempest went immediately up to her room, collapsing in exhaustion on her bed.

Thursday rolled around, and she spent the day in the library, working under Raven's watchful eye, on Rhydian's history project. Far before she was done, it was time to go back to her dorm room, for the night. Meals that day were salad and sandwiches. On one of the walls of the library, was written, 'it is possible to teach focus, but teaching attentiveness is impossible, as impossible as teaching freedom from fear.' Beneath that, someone had scribbled a translation 'no matter how experienced the teacher is, teaching can only be successful if the student is eager and able to learn.' She had stared up at the wall, trying to understand the saying. That night, the words came back to her and she became determined to take learning seriously.

CHAPTER 24

A RUDE AWAKENING

FRIDAY, FAR BEFORE DAYBREAK, WHILE SHE was still lying fast asleep, there was a pounding on her door. "Get up Tempest!" Came Sarge's voice. She rolled out of bed as he knocked. She opened the door, confused. He pulled her out, shoving her down the stairs. She stumbled into the main hall, where she was met by Rebel, Laura and the rest of the Beta teams. "Move move move!" Came Sarge's voice, sending them out into the darkness of predawn. Most of the others were also barefoot in their pyjamas. A few were dressed in their flight suits, as though they knew this was coming. They ran outside, being lead by one of the Alpha teams. Through the city, out to the woods, Sarge had them run around in circles. Over and under logs until noon. The men were mostly wearing pants. Women, like Tempest, wore tank tops and pants. They were all soaked when Sarge had them jog into the tree tower to eat.

"Well done, all of you." He called looking around the tree. "Eat, then go clean the dragons. I'll be taking your teams up to gryphon ride." He said, dismissing them to eat the field rations that were handed out.

They headed down to clean the dragons. Eventually, their team was called up and taken out to fly. Unlike when Jason had taken them up, they were permitted to fly where they wished. Sarge stood on the tree top, calling orders through their helmets. "Tempest turn to the left, Rebel pull up your gonna nick the wall, Laura drop your altitude!" After several hours of having instructions yelled at them, they were told to land and clean the gryphons, who were soaked in sweat. Tempest and the others brushed the fur and feathers carefully. Tempest's gryphon leaned it's head against her shoulder, as she groomed the creature. Once they had completed their task, they were dismissed for the day.

The threesome headed off to the showers, cleaning up. Magically, their laundry always appeared exactly where they needed it. When Tempest asked Laura about this strange phenomenon, "It's magic" she said, as though that explained everything. Tempest grumbled but let it go.

CHAPTER 25

GUESTS

T HEY SEEMED TO TAKE EVERYTHING FOR granted here, dismissing it as magic. Her curiosity, however, would not let the matter go when they arrived at the magic tower. Tempest split off, turning down the hall to go find Raven. She knocked on her office door. "Ma'am, I umm have a request and a question." Tempest said as she walked in. Raven nodded, signalling that she should keep talking. "May, umm, could Rebel and Laura come to my home, spend the weekend hanging out. It would help with the story that I go to a normal school?" She asked softly looking at Raven.

Raven glanced up from her paperwork. "You are to behave, be careful." She ordered seriously, then she smiled, "and have fun! Now what is your question?"

Tempest chuckled, "why does everyone just dismiss stuff as 'it's magic'?' It seems, if they don't know how something works, they just say 'it's magic' and it's dismissed as normal?"

Raven chucked, "it is the way it is here. It is taken as the way things are. I remember a time, when it wasn't this way. When we had to work for everything. Some have lost this understanding, that things were not always this easy. It would be good for your fellow students to do chores around your home, in order to learn this." Raven explained to her, smiling "teach them and have fun." She said dismissing Tempest. She nodded in understanding, then turned, leaving the office, running to find her friends.

Laura and Rebel were in the dinning hall, already eating. She sat down to join them, pulling the plate they had made for her closer. "So who wants to take a trip?" She asked, smiling from ear to ear. She took a bite of her salad, admiring the confused looks they were giving her.

"No way, Sarge would never agree." Laura laughed, as she looked at Tempest, waiting for her to spill the beans for Rebel. Laura always put things together faster.

Tempest only shook her head, "who says I went to Sarge." She ate her salad, still grinning like a cat. "I asked Raven!"

Rebel chucked, "well, we'd best go find human world clothes. Wardrobe room?" He looked to Laura, who nodded.

"Soon, when we are done eating. Tempest you can come too. I think you'll enjoy this," Laura told Tempest. Ten minutes later, they were taking her to the storage room, before Rhydian's room. Down near the far wall, there were racks of clothes from all different time periods. From medieval court dresses, and suits of armour, to jeans and t-shirts to leather armour and all other sorts.

Tempest wandered the racks, while Rebel and Laura found clothes for the weekend. She didn't notice when they vanished to a changing area. She was too engrossed in picking up a well oiled bow. The pair came back, causing Tempest to drop the bow, surprised that they looked so normal. Rebel wore gym shorts and a T-shirt with nine planets on it, while Laura wore jeans and a gym shirt like Rebels. They both carried duffel bags, with what she assumed were changes of clothes. They were dressed like teens, though their cat like features remained. "Is there anything you can do about the, umm fur colouring and ears?"

Laura chuckled, "don't worry, we will appear human to normal people. No one in your house believes in magic right?"

She shook her head, "doubtful, they are so founded in reality." Looking around at Laura and Rebel, she smiled, she was looking forward to this. "These weapons, they are all still maintained, why?" She asked curiously.

"They are maintained because they are still in use. When the occasion arises, as it did during the great war, when we were invaded. It does us no harm to be prepared." She said picking the bow up. She ran her hand along with wood, checking it for damage. Then she placed it back on it's hanging space. "We should be fine then, right Rebel. Theoretically, if they don't believe we should appear as they would expect?"

Rebel nodded in agreement, then explained. "That is the way it worked during the war. I specialize in war history. Are we using your portal?"

"Yup, let's get going. This is my first weekend back. I want to be there before my folks get home." Tempest said, as they ran up the stairs to her room. They crammed into the circle, then Tempest clicked her watch. They were engulfed in white light as they were transported to her room, in her folks house.

CHAPTER 26

HUMAN WORLD

S HE LOOKED AT REBEL AND LAURA as they stepped out. They appeared human, unless she looked hard. "Well, this is my room." Tempest said and walked them through to the kitchen, showing them around the house. They were sitting around on the couch, watching television, when her brother walked in. "Hey little sister! Folks are out getting groceries, how are you doing Tempest?" He asked looking to the others, "hello!"

"Hey Steve, I'm good and you?" Tempest asked jumping up to hug him.

Wrapping his arm around her, he turned her to her friends, "I'm fine, now who do we have here?"

"Umm, these are my classmates, Rebel and Laura." Tempest sat back on the couch. Steve dropped down in a chair across from her.

"Nice to meet you both!" He said, reaching across to shake their hands.

Rebel took his hand, after Laura "nice to meet you as well." He said starring him down. Tempest saw their hands tightening, trying to outdo each other. Laura chucked, her stripes and fangs showing for an instant across her face. Steve showed no sign of noticing. The guys released hands.

"Your bunking with me, Rebel. Laura can bunk with you, Tempest." Steve said as car doors slammed, announcing her folks arrival. Steve and Tempest went out helping bring in the groceries. Once everyone was in, her parents were thrilled to meet her classmates. The weekend went by quietly, with no huge issues. When it came to doing the dishes, sweeping and helping with the laundry, they were amazed with how long the chores went, however they were happy enough to help.

CHAPTER 27

✦

STEVE'S SECRET

MONDAY MORNING CAME AND THEY WERE getting ready to leave. Her folks had already left. Steve had remained at home, claiming to be sick. However, he didn't let them out of his sight.

Her brother sat at her desk, watching them. He was waiting for them to leave. "When do you catch your bus?" He asked, playing with the portal watch, holding the chain, letting it twist through the air.

"Umm, bus is late Steve, shouldn't you be resting?" She asked nervously, her gaze resting on the watch.

He shook his head. "You can have your little 'bus pass' here back on one condition." He said, letting the watch twist in the air. He stood walking over to Tempest. He grabbed her wrist and he turned it over. The paw print showing bright green. "You must come back. I know our grandmother didn't, I've met her too."

Tempest looked at him, shocked. "How long have you known?"

He chuckled, "since I saw the scars on your ankle." He admitted, tossing the watch to her. He looked over at Rebel and Laura. "Watch over her you guys." He said, before leaving the room. Tempest starred after him, too flabbergasted to speak. She looked at her team, and motioned for them to follow her. They crowded into the portal ring and teleported through, hurrying to their own rooms to get changed for school.

CHAPTER 28

ATLANTIS

T HEY ALL MET UP AT THE magic tower entrance hall, then sprinted towards the tree tower to start class. Sarge stood waiting, "out to the obstacle course" he shouted, as they arrived. They spent the rest of the day, running themselves ragged. They started on the ground course, then moving up to the next level. Sweat poured from their skins. Dusk came and they went into the showers, cleaning up and getting changed. They ate supper, then went to their rooms. Tempest checked her pockets, making sure she had her map stuffed into her pocket. After Sarge's unexpected work-out, she wasn't taking any chances. She unlaced her boots, setting them next to her bed. Her pants, she laid on the end of her bed. Her jacket was on the back of her chair. When she was sure she was ready, she laid down on her bed and fell into a deep sleep.

Soon enough, she was fast asleep, lost in her dreams. She was unable to tell what was reality, and what was false. Then, it happened. She saw a huge floating island, soaring in the clouds. Dragons, bats, gryphons and indescribable creatures, soared around it. Spiralling towers of gold and stone stuck into the sky. Water poured over the edges, into the clouds below, the floating island. In the centre, was a mountain. On top of the mountain, stood a castle. The towers and spires, were attached to a large castle. Tall walls protected it from invaders. As she looked closer, she observed a ballon, attached to one of the towers. The ballon, had a schooner attached beneath it. Tempest tried to get closer, but found the wind controlled her flight. She was floating away from where the city floated. She flew away from the city, being blown off course.

She sat up in her bed, staring at the door. She climbed out of bed, placing her feet in her boots. Lacing them up, Tempest climbed the stairs. She climbed up to the trap door, pushing it open. Instantly, she was drenched, as water poured over her head. She coughed up water, as she made her way through the trap door. Climbing onto the roof, looking up at the sky. There, floating high above were clouds, water poured from the clouds like a waterfall. She shook her head, then noticed other people had followed her up.

Rebel stood nearby, "inconceivable!" He expressed, as he looked at the clouds. Water had flattened his fur. Raven looked at him, as he shot shot Tempest a look, telling her to stay silent. "Back downstairs, everyone, it's just a storm." She ushered the students back below, through the trapdoor. "Go back to your beds." She practically stuffed them down the stairs, one after another.

Rebel ducked off at her floor, following Tempest to her room. She moved to go inside, turning to Rebel, "okay, enough with the following, what's up?"

Rebel looked at her, "we have to go! We can fly up there, before they know we're gone!"

Tempest shook her head, "why do you want us to fly into a storm?" It didn't sound remotely fun, just wet and cold. If thunder started, it would be like the electric challenge all over again.

He shook his head, "that's not any rain storm....that's Atlantis, where they made the peace treaties. Only the air knights, an elite group of the guards, a few trespassers, and a few crazy students, over the years have been up there since. Come on, it's our job to break rules, its expected, we're students! We are at the flight school, to become air knights, the elite, the best! The guard of Emor is ok and everything, but the Air Knights are amazing."

"Rebel, I don't want to be expelled and sent back to the normal world, kicked out of magic. Besides, what about Laura?" She asked exasperated. She watched the other students walk down the halls, they all seemed to be chattering about the legend of Atlantis.

Rebel grinned, "she's waiting for us with three gryphons, on the edge of the of the city. Besides, we won't be the only ones going up, or trying to. It's like a right of passage, come with us Tempest." He begged watching her. "We've been planing for this for months, you're part of our team!"

"Fine Rebel, let's go." She sighed. Of course she had alternative motives for agreeing to go up. She had just realized that ballon ship was attached to the floating city. "I thought Atlantis was lost under the seas...." She followed him down the stairs.

He laughed, "no, no that's what we told the humans. Atlantis was the first magical city. You see, in the beginning, all people could all do magic. People chose to stop using magic, they became the first humans, their children were born without it, eventually. Atlantis became a magical sanctuary. The mages of the time, put a floating spell on the island. They gave their lives to create a way for us to protect our city and people."

"Are there weapons up there?" Tempest stopped dead in her tracks turning to Rebel.

He shook his head, "not traditional weapons, that I know of. However, there is supposed to be plenty of battle magic, stored in the armoury. That's why only the Air knights are permitted up there. Of course, knowledge is power according to the Air knights, so that could just be knowledge up there." She leapt down to the next landing. Rebel followed, as quickly as he could, while Tempest took the steps. Three at a time, practically throwing herself down them. "What's the matter Tempest?" He asked chasing after her, bouncing off the walls.

"Orben! Vlad's brother is up there!" She said not bothering to turn to talk to him.

Rebel grabbed her arm, "no way, he's not even aloud to fly. Not since he got kicked out. Relax, no flying critter would permit him to fly! They wouldn't trust him."

She shook her head, "he's got a sky ship!" Tempest was shaking as she ran on. Adrenaline coursed through her. She ducked down the last couple stairs, skidding to a halt in front of Raven.

Where do you think you two are going?" She asked as Rebel ran into Tempest. Raven caught the pair, supporting them.

"I just wanted to play in the water." Tempest lied lamely, realizing she was still in soaked clothes from the tower top, "you know splash in the puddles and stuff."

"Don't stay out there to long" Raven told her, then looked at Rebel. "Not you, back up to your bed. Rebel, your father would be furious. He would have me running his obstacle course if I let his favourite son get sick. You know how the flight commander gets." Rebel grumbled as he turned and headed back up the stairs.

Tempest looked back over her shoulder at Raven. Raven watched Tempest from the front doorway, as she bounced in the puddles, trying to look as though she was having fun. Silently, she cursed herself for the lack of thought on her part, coming out without her flight suit. At least she had her map, stuffed in her pocket. She splashed her way through the puddles, around the corner and out of view. Now, how to find Laura, she had the gryphons. Tempest dug into her pocket and pulled out the map card. "Guide me to Laura please," she requested. The map instantly came to life, guiding her out into the city. She traveled out through the side streets and to the edge of the city. Laura stood with three gryphons, waiting impatiently.

She waved Tempest over, "where's Rebel?" She asked looking around nervously.

"Raven caught him as we were on our way out. She didn't seem happy that he would sneak out. I don't suppose you've got any dry clothes?" Tempest asked, looking at the gryphons hesitantly. She would freeze if she had to fly with wet clothes.

Laura shook her head, "sorry, it didn't occur to me. Were you followed?" She asked as Tempest walked over to her. Laura tapped her shoulder, muttering under her breath. Instantly her clothes were dry and warm.

"Why didn't I think of that?" She asked, looking down at her clothes and boots. She wiggled her toes, "even my socks are dry!"

She chuckled, "you're new to magic. With your luck, you would have sucked all the water out of your body. I don't have Vlad's gift for keeping people alive. So, I wouldn't have let you try anyway!" Tempest approached the gryphons. She kept her hands at her sides, her palms facing the gryphon, trying to look non-threatening.

"Let's go!" Tempest said and climbed on one gryphon, Laura took another. They flew up, towards the clouds. The wall of water fell ahead of them. Circling around slowly, they built altitude until they were above the island. Atlantis lay below them. She could barely make out the buildings. Fog covered much of the city, though the gryphons didn't seem to have a problem. They flew through the arches and around the streets. They were about to land when, Tempest saw Orben's air ship, floating high above. Tempest gently nudged her gryphon, directing her to the east, into the castle courtyard, where they landed. "Laura, go tell Raven." She ordered, leaping off her gryphon and running to one of the towers. She could see figures disembarking from the airship, on the tower landing. Tempest didn't look back to see if Laura was going to follow her orders. She she'd go get Raven and reinforcements. If there were weapons up here, Tempest had to stop him. He'd destroy everyone, starting with her own city, if he had a chance. Since she had taken off to the human world and avoided becoming the vampires pet he had hated her. Vlad had warned her to be on her guard. He wanted to shatter her world.

CHAPTER 29

CAPTURED

TEMPEST RAN INTO THE CASTLE, GOING straight up the stairs. She felt the ground change direction and pick up speed. She fell against one wall, then down the stairs, landing on the stone floor. Tempest pushed herself off the stone floor of the entry hall. She heard foot steps barreling down the stairs. She pushed herself off the ground, as she heard a cold menacing voice. "Make sure the citadel is secure!" the voice yelled. She tried to sneak into a shadow, begging it to hide her. No such luck. Two huge men came running down the stairs, they resembled grizzly bears crossed with humans. They each grabbed an arm, hoisting her into the air. "The master will want this one!" Said one of the men. "She's the human who stopped the skeletons!"

The other nodded, "I'll take her you finish the sweep!" The smaller bear man nodded, releasing her arm. He lumbered off, as the larger one dragged her up the stairs. When they reached the top, she was taken into a room with a large globe sitting in the middle of the room. An old man lay on the floor next to it, bleeding from a crossbow bolt in his chest. Dead eyes bore into Tempests, while she looked around the room, hunting for anything that could be used as a weapon.

Orben stood next to the globe, his arms behind his back. On the other side of the globe, stood a man in a black suit, a cane in one hand and a whip tied at his hip. Tempest's eyes traveled up, she noticed he looked human. His mouth was a tight thin line and his eyes were reptilian. "Ah Tempest, how nice of you to join us." His tongue darted out, tasting the air like a snake.

"I am the dark one, the master of evil, Telemont!" He said as she was brought forward to him.

"Well Telemont, I am Tempest." She said glaring at the man, "and you are going to leave this place now!" She tried to sound braver then she felt, practically shaking in fear. She was starting to freeze, just standing there beneath his gaze.

Telemont smiled his evil smile, "yes, you are so fierce. I am sure, 'go away' works on all your fears. However, I am so much more than that. What do you think Orben? Lock her up or throw her off Atlantis?" Telemont watched her like she was a specimen under a microscope.

Orben grinned, "sir, let me drain her. I'll make her pay for stopping your skeletons. Then we'll throw her body over the edge." Telemont nodded and motioned for the grizzly man to take her away.

The bear man dragged her down the stairs, to the dungeons. Tempest was thrown into a dark cell and left her in darkness. She leaped to her feet. Spinning around, she slammed against the heavy wooden door. There had to be a way out, there was always a way out. She tried pushing then pulling, she slammed her fists and the door was still unwilling to open. Tempest grumbled and felt her way around the dark room. Finally, she sat down in the corner, near the door. Her eyes closed, she concentrated, thinking about fire. She knew if she could manipulate the air around the door, to dry out, she could make fire to remove the moisture. She also knew, however, she had to protect herself. Tempest asked the air around her to remain damp. However, this multitasking was beyond her.

She collapsed passing out on the cold damp floor. Tempest sat up, slowly realizing what she had tried was too much for her. She had to think smaller. Old wood meant equally old hinges. She placed her hand where the hinges were located on the outside. She tried oxidizing the already rusted metal. She heard what sounded like sand, trickle to the floor. Tempest gave the door a slight push. The door angled open, the lock acting as a hinge.

Once she was out of her cell, she crept down the hallway, going back the way she had been dragged. She faltered for a moment, thinking that perhaps she should wait for reinforcements. It was foolish to go forward, but she had to find out what Orben and Telemont were doing. Tempest decided she would report back, once she had information. She continued up to the control room, to find plans or a map. Something concrete she could take to

Raven. Upon reaching the door to the control room, she crouched down listening at the keyhole, though she heard no sound within.

She opened the door, enough to peer around. Seeing no one was present, she ran inside. She moved quickly, to a desk behind the globe. The desk top was empty. Franticly, she opened drawers. She turned, looking at a wall behind her. The wall was plastered with maps and papers, she tore these from the walls. Then she rolled as many maps as she could, along with sheets of paper, before stuffing them into a bag on the floor.

She took as much time as she dared when she heard voices approaching and knew it was time to leave. She went to the window. Yanking it open, she tossed the bag out and dove after it. The ground approached, faster then she thought possible. "Okay, slow down," She told herself. The air slowed her down, enough that all she did was scrape her hands and knees. Her slacks were no where near as tough as her flight suit. She pushed herself up from the ground, running through the streets, leaving a trail of blood. Past the buildings, houses and stores. All stood abandoned. She skidded around the corner, reaching the edge of the island. She leapt. She whistled the call for the gryphon. Before she fell far, she had her breath knocked from her lungs, she had landed on the gryphons back. The gryphon fell a little, loosing altitude. He circled under the great floating city, soaking the pair from the water pouring down.

They had traveled far from Emor, while they had been on Atlantis. The city lights were no longer in view. Tempest wrapped her arms around her gryphons neck, tucking her head into the feathers. The gryphon picked up speed, sensing her urgency. They flew faster than she had dared to go before. When they arrived at Emor, Tempest directed the gryphon to the magic tower. They landed within the courtyard. Raven was waiting out front, with Sarge and Laura.

CHAPTER 30

RETALIATION

TEMPEST DISMOUNTED. GOING TO RAVEN, SHE took the bag, handing it to the headmistress. "I know I'm grounded," She admitted. Then she looked at Sarge. "Sir, I must report, Orben was in Atlantis." She said standing at attention. He nodded as Raven pulled the paper work out.

"Sarge, these papers are indeed from the Atlantis control room. Tempest we need to know if you activated anything." Raven demanded rolling the papers back up.

"Nothing. I activated nothing. However, I saw Orben. He is working with a man named Telemont," she stared at their eyes, willing them to believe her.

Raven nodded slowly, she knew of Orben's desire to cause chaos. He had once attended this very school. He had been one of the top students, until it was discovered that he was trying to form his own personal army. Raven looked at the commander. "Wake up the squads, get them to track the air ship." She looked back at Tempest, "get Jason and Vlad. Meet in the Rhydian's lab in ten minutes." Sarge whistled, and a large bat swooped in. He raised his hand and the bat grabbed it, carrying him towards the Nest.

Tempest didn't bother with her map. She ran through the streets, to Vlad and Jason's house. She banged on the front door, which opened after a few moments. Vlad stumbled from his rooms, "why are you trying to break the door down, Tempest?" He was furious. He was wearing black dress pants and a white dress shirt, as though getting ready for a dinner party.

"Quick, get Jason! Orben is in Atlantis. Raven wants us at Rhydian's lab, now!" Tempest said between breaths. Vlad turned, going up the stairs. A minute later, he came down, dragging Jason. He had one boot on and his arm sticking out of the wrong sleeve. His hair was a mess, but it usually was. Vlad held Jason's helmet and took his jacket. Jason put his other boot on as he hit the bottom stair. He took his jacket off, putting it back on right this time.

"Just got home." He said, as an excuse. Vlad handed him his helmet and they left, going to the magic school. They jumped onto a large rug that spun them up to Rhydian's floor at emergency speed. They jumped off the rug before it stopped and ran into his work room.

Raven stood waiting for them, she wasted no time with pleasantries. "I'm sending you three in. Vlad, Orben's your brother. See if you can talk to him. Jason, if he fails, you take Orben down, anyway you can. Tempest, I'm sending you because you seem to have a lucky streak. You proved to be a good team in the past. Go fly up and bring him back, dead or alive. Preferably alive, I want him to stand trial. However, that is not always possible, right Jason?" He grinned and nodded. He knew when he was being sent as an assassin. "Just stop him got it? Stop Atlantis first before it wanders off course or crashes that's the last thing we need a flying island hitting us when we aren't looking." Jason, that's your primary mission."

Suddenly, Tempest was very cold. She had forgotten that her friends were over three hundred years old. How many lives had they been sent to take. What did that make her? Would she kill when she was called to? Would she become like them, enjoying the hunt and chase, those few minutes before the life drained from her prey? She wondered as she looked to Raven, who shook her head. Not for the first time, did Tempest wonder if she could read her mind.

Rhydian handed the three of them black flight suits, "tap the wrists and gloves slide out." He instructed them, "new invention." He handed Vlad and Tempest helmets, which they placed on their heads. "Need one?" He asked Jason, holding one out.

"No I prefer mine." Jason led them to the top of the school, where he called three gryphons. They mounted quickly, and were flown to the flight school. Once there, Jason lead them to the bats who roosted in nearby branches, giving them a crash course in flying. "These are racers," Jason said.

He looked toward Tempest and Vlad, "they are faster, more agile. Usually, they are used for mail delivery or emergencies. They are also trained to trust more easily." They nodded, paying close attention. Vlad looked terrified, he obviously didn't like the idea of flying. Jason put a hand on his shoulder, "if we stop Orben, I'm sure your gods will forgive you." Vlad did not look any happier. "Vampires are only supposed to fly under their own power. It's against their code to use other methods like gryphons and dragons." He explained to Tempest, as Vlad stepped away, saying a silent prayer to his gods.

They climbed onto the bats, laying flat against the bat's back. The fur tickled Tempest's hands. In front of her, it's ears swivelled, the bat was quiet cute, when you got over the fact that it was just that, a bat. "Don't worry guys, they will follow my orders, I hope." Jason muttered softly, seeing their fear.

Jason's bat took off and Vlad's followed. Then Tempest's dove off, soaring faster than she had thought possible. The cold air bit at the skin on the back of her hands, before she remembered the gloves. She tapped one wrist and then the other. The gloves slid over her hands as a liquid, then solidifying as they covered her hands.

"Shadow hawks!" Jason yelled. A cloud of shadows, forming hawks, flew between them and Atlantis. The trio slammed through, ducking and weaving, as they approached the castle of Atlantis. The bats barely slowed them, but they had done their job, buying time.

CHAPTER 31

RETURN OF THE SKELETONS

WITH ALL THEIR SPEED, THEY WERE still too late. They watched as Orben's airship took off, away from them, vanishing in a flash. Jason lead them towards Atlantis he knew what the others did not that it was startlingly off course and on it's present trajectory it was going straight for the human world. They circled the tower once. On the second lap of the tower, the bats latched onto landing pegs protruding from the tower, above a balcony. Vlad looked to Jason, "lead the way." Jason nodded, leading them down the hallways, to the control room. They found the doors locked, which slowed them down as they had been warded against magic. Tempest silently thanked her brother, for teaching her to pick locks one summer. When the click was finally heard, the door sprang open. They found the control room globe, laying in pieces, all around the room. Vlad looked around disappointed, "we can't guide it, not without the globe."

Jason shook his head in disgust. "Think we could manually steer the sky drive, or at least stop it?"

Vlad hesitated, then nodded. "Perhaps avoid crashing, if we're lucky. Okay, you and Tempest take out either the back drive, that should stop it, or one of the side drives, so it goes in circles."

Jason nodded, "and you, Vlad, have to try to pick up Orben's trail. I can do more damage to the engines than you, if it comes to that."

Tempest looked around the control room. "What are we waiting for, snow to fall? Orben's trail is getting colder and we are getting closer to the human border." Vlad nodded, leaping out the window and onto his bat. He quickly vanished from sight. He seemed to have made peace with aided flight, at least for a time.

Jason lead her down the stairs and through the corridors. "We'll take out a side engine. That way, we can still steer, hopefully. Rather then compromising the whole system, and crashing the island." He explained as they ran for the right side engine. "Circles are better than crashing." Jason said more to himself then her. "The back engine would be the obvious one. There would, theoretically, be more traps there."

They reached the right engine room, only to find a troll skeleton, standing before them. The troll ran at them, swinging a work bench like a club. "Not another skeleton!" Tempest groaned ducking. Jason jumped into the air, to avoid the bench hitting him. He landed on the end of the bench. The troll's skull turned to him, empty eye sockets staring. Tempest shivered, launching herself at the rib cage. Sliding through a pair of ribs, she grabbed the spine, pulling it with her out the back. Tempest heard a crack. The spine came free and the troll skeleton fell to pieces. "YUCK!" She dropped the spine to the ground.

Jason laughed with relief. He watched her wipe her gloves on her pants. "Nice move, how'd you think of that?" He had dropped to the ground, when the skeleton fell to pieces.

She shrugged, "figured it needed it's spine to hold it together, thought perhaps it'd work," she said gazing up at the engine.

The engine was a massive fish tank attached to pipes, leading off in all directions. "Water ferns, they produce the water. These little guppy looking fish, are helium fish. They breath in water and out comes helium. The helium goes through the island, acting as a propellent. It's an ancient system. The idea is supposedly based on the roman aqueducts. Creating it, took the lives of several mages." He explained as they approached. "It has never been duplicated, because it took the lives of all involved. The cost was to high."

"If we pull the pipes at the top or find shut off valves, we could temporarily turn this off." She said, gazing at the maze of pipes above her head. Jason picked her up, standing her on his shoulders. Ten minuets of frantic searching later, she'd still found no valves to turn the system off.

Jason put her down, then reached up and tried to pull the pipes apart. He shook his head and transformed to his large werewolf form. He swiped at the pipes, his claws slicing them to pieces. He returned to his human form. "I didn't want to resort to that, it just makes more repair work." They jogged up the hallway. "I hope Rhydian doesn't get sick, flying in circles." He chuckled as Vlad came into sight. He was slamming his fists into the hard brick wall, they left no mark in the stone. "Vlad stop that. You'll only hurt yourself, this stone is indestructible.

"No luck, he must have developed a new type of teleport device. He vanished into nothing" Vlad admitted unhappily. "No trail, at least nothing that flying rat could pick up." He turned his hands over, his knuckles bloody. He shook his hands and blood flew, off splattering the walls, his hands healed. The stone itself seemed to suck the blood into it's mortar.

Jason looked at him, "we should find and disable the traps your brother left for Rhydian and his team. They couldn't see a trap if it was marked with a black cartoon X. They are so easily distracted by technology. Raven will have new orders for us, eventually." As they moved through the city, more teams slowly started arriving, helping clear the city. When they finished their sector, the trio went to the control room.

CHAPTER 32

BEST LAID PLANS

RAVEN, RHYDIAN AND SARGE WERE IN the control room. Rhydian sat on the ground, trying to put the pieces of the globe back together. Raven stood next to the body, now covered in a sheet, shaking her head. Sarge stood watching Rhydian, as though he could make him work faster by watching him. Tempest moved forward, to help, as Jason explained what they had done and how Tempest had taken down a skeleton troll.

Vlad reported that he had failed to catch Orben. Rhydian turned around, "he must have taken a teleportation device." He looked at Tempest, both eyes focused on her. "Can you form a mental picture of what this place should look like?" Tempest nodded, forming a mental picture of what she had seen. Rhydian tapped her forehead, "this is going to take me weeks. My repair spell isn't working on these pieces, which means, I have to build it from these scraps. Technology no one has studied in thousands of years, I have to rebuild."

Raven nodded, "then it's a good thing I have other techies working on installing shut off valves, so we can manually steer Atlantis. It has been a long time since it has been fully occupied. Sarge, you're in charge of the defence of Emor. Jason I'd like to keep you here, because of your defensive training. I know you've never defended something on this scale before, but it's either you or Sarge and he's needed in Emor. I'm also pulling Rain from retirement, to help run things on the ground. We'll send out all the teams. Sarge, the bats are to act as boarder guards. Get the gryphons to track and the dragons to check the towns and cities. Leave running Emor to Rain, you concentrate on your troops. Tempest if the worst happens, do you think humans could handle magic being revealed?" Tempest found herself shaking her head thinking, 'humans are not ready for magic. What about those who couldn't see it? No, it's not right to force it on them."

She nodded, "okay. So that's teams to hunt, to patrol, to check, warn the towns and villages. Jason, use what you must to fortify Atlantis. I'll be giving everyone this order, I think you need to hear it, Tempest. Do not engage Telemont and Orben, you are not ready and they are killers." Raven watched Tempest until she nodded.

"OK, no contact. We find, watch and send someone to tell you where he is," Tempest stated.

Raven looked at her as seriously as she could. "You come back and tell us where he is. You don't tell someone else, you come back. I don't need to hear your grandmother complain about you being murdered senselessly. I also don't want to lose our newest human." Raven ordered waiting on Tempest to answer.

Tempest nodded, "yes ma'am," she turned to leave.

Jason touched her shoulder, "be carful kid." He told her looking concerned.

She glared, determined "we will find him, and I will come back to report. But when we take him down, I want to be the one to do it is that clear?" Jason looked surprised as Tempest turned to Raven. "It's my world he's threatening, my family. I want to take him down."

Raven watched her, for what felt like an eternity. "Okay, but we all attack as a group. We can't afford mistakes. You'll get your chance, if it can be arranged, that's all I can promise." Tempest nodded, turning to leave, Rebel and Laura joined her as she walked down the corridor. They walked out to the courtyard where the gryphons had been landing. They gathered saddles and supplies from the side of the wall and fit their gear to the gryphons and launched out of the courtyard.

CHAPTER 33

HUNTING

THE GRYPHONS WERE NOT NEARLY AS fast as the racing bats, but they could pick up scents from miles away. The gryphons turned east, flying toward the ocean, according to Rebel. She didn't understand how that was possible, it didn't match her worlds geography. If they were in the human world, they would have been over the ocean by now. When she asked Laura explained by telling her, the magic world had it's own geography. They let the gryphons fly where they would. They didn't land for the first two days. The night of the second day, Tempest decided they would land for the night, everyone needed rest. They set up hammocks in the highest branches of the trees. Rebel didn't think it was safe to camp on the ground.

Tempest was uncertain of where they were, in relation to the human world. They all knew whom they were chasing and couldn't take the chance of landing on the ground. They didn't know what traps Orben and Telemont had lain or if they had unleashed more skeletons. Rebel had been studying Atlantis, he told them of the hunting hounds. They were a ghost demon dog, that could track it's prey anywhere. They were kept on Atlantis nether living nor dead. They were a weapon.

Thursday was an early start, they had breakfast on the fly. Around noon, they spotted a speck in the distance. "Think that's it?" Tempest asked, looking at Laura.

Laura didn't answer for a few moments. "We'll get a closer look but it might be." Her eyes were far better then her Tempests. Tempest didn't want to go back and tell them where Orben was only to have him teleport away. They flew on. By noon, they saw it was an airship, like the one Orben had been seen using.

Tempest kept them high above the ship, in the clouds. She looked to the others, motioning for them to land on a cloud. As they landed, Laura dug a small trench in one of the clouds, asking the cloud to fill it with water for the gryphons to drink. "If he's got a teleport device, he could leave at any time. I say we act fast and hit him hard. We can't lose this chance." Laura glared, "I know I promised Raven but do you want to lose him? We take out Orben, if we run into him first, the teleport device if we don't." Tempest instructed looking to the others for approval. The pair nodded, waiting for darkness to cover their attack.

As darkness fell, they plummeted towards the ship. The gryphons stopped, hovering above the ship. They avoided landing to prevent the claws from puncturing the ballon. Silently, they climbed down, using the ropes that held the ballon to the ship. Tempest slid down the lines, her feet lightly touched the deck, with a soft thud. They had made a plan while waiting for sundown on the cloud above. They would look for the teleport device. Down the stairs, they walked silently, it was a ghost ship, no one abroad. Once inside, Tempest saw a figure, hunched over, sitting on the hard wooden floor. As they got closer, she saw the figure was blindfolded, chains held him to the walls. The figure looked as though he'd been beaten to a pulp. Most of his skin was bruised, what wasn't bruised was sliced.

CHAPTER 34

FINDING SCOTT

TEMPEST PULLED THE BLINDFOLD OFF AND gasped. It was a barely conscious Scott. He blinked, looking at her, puzzled "hello Tempest." She motioned for him to stay quiet, he didn't. "You know, usually my hallucinations are more talkative. Sometimes you and Jason rescue me. Other times, I rescue you by teleporting us out. Usually, you just die though," he admitted. "Orben or Telemont kill you a lot."

She looked at him, watching his eyes. He was delirious from thirst and hunger. She was willing to bet blood loss was an issue also. "Scott, snap out of it. We're here to rescue you." She went to check the chains, looking for how to undo them. Tempest saw then, that the bolt went right through his wrists healed into place. When he moved, the wounds reopened healing almost as quickly.

They heard footsteps approaching, coming down the stairs. She quickly replaced the blindfold. Her team spread out, into the shadows, hiding among the rafters and crates laying around. Orben walked in and over to Scott, who was giggling like he'd lost his mind. Orben pulled the blindfold off, issuing Scott an order, "teleport boy!"

The world shifted, as they were pulled to another place. Tempest felt queazy, shaking her head to clear it. Orben replaced the blindfold, going back upstairs. She crept over to Scott taking the blindfold from him.

"Your still here." He said surprised, "I never take my hallucinations with me."

Tempest nodded, "yes well, that's because I'm real and here to rescue you." She tentatively held his wrist. "Can you teleport just yourself?" She asked looking for a way to undo the chains from him, then the wall. They had been drilled into the beams. She hunted for weak points, anything to undo them. "Rebel check his wrists, see if there is anything you can do."

Scott looked at her his eyes slowly focusing. "We've had this discussion before, the answer is still no. I don't know how it works let alone how to control it. I teleport everything touching my skin, no control."

She glanced at Rebel who shook his head. "Well then, this is going to hurt." He only nodded as Tempest undid the nut holding the bolt in place. He whimpered, but didn't cry out as she finally pulled the bolt out. She started on the other hand, when she had him freed he looked pale and sicker. "Do you have the strength to teleport?" She asked watching him. Laura and Rebel had come forward, holding his wounds closed, binding them as well as they could on the spot.

Scott nodded, they were suddenly standing around Scott in the werewolf summer camp. Tempest wasn't picky, he'd gotten them out of the airship. However, it was late summer and everyone was in Emor for the winter. With no help in sight she wasn't sure how much she could do.

CHAPTER 35

WHEN ALL ELSE FAILS

REBEL WORKED ON HEALING SCOTT'S WOUNDS. Knitting bones, muscles and ligaments all into place. Tempest went to one of the huts, laying her hand on the door. The paw tattoo on her wrist glowed as the door swung open. She set the hut for them to crash in, Laura came in. "Rebel says not to move Scotts hands for seventy-two hours and no magic for at least forty-eight. The kid was through hell, he's just realizing he's free. Rebel is trying to get some water and food in him but he just seems to want to talk to you. If you want, I'll help you finish up in here so you can go convince him to eat." She helped make up camp beds. Tempest was hoping Rebel could get Scott to eat without her. Her stomach felt sick at what Orben had done to the boy.

"Yea, okay just three beds, eh? One of us should keep watch for Orben. Who knows where we were when Scott teleported us down here." Tempest did not want him sneaking up on them.

When they finished, Tempest went out, helping move Scott into the hut. They set him on a bed. He looked around fifteen years old, thanks to the gift the wolf mother had given him. Tempest reminded herself he was closer to ten, as he babbled her ears off about how Orben had kidnapped him. She took a piece of dried meat and stuffed it into his mouth. "EAT!" She ordered him shaking her head in frustration. "I'm only going to answer your questions and talk if you eat and drink," she told him sternly. He nodded and started eating. Between bites, he asked where Jason was, what was going on with her, why she was there. She could have sworn he only knew five words: who, what, when, where and how. "Look, we are safe Scott, that's all that matters. Jason's up on Atlantis with Raven keeping it safe. My grandmother is running Emor with Rebel's dad." She told him of how they had picked up Vlad and then destroyed the skeletons that had invaded the lake. Tempest told him about how she had chosen to come to school in Emor, about Rhydian's work room. Talking until he fell asleep snoring quietly.

She shook her head, laying Scott down, gently wrapping him in a blanket. Rebel had first watch and Laura had gone to find firewood. Eventually, Laura came back with a rabbit and firewood. She took the second watch, cooking the rabbit. Tempest was woken for the third shift, she sat down outside the hut. Listening to the woods around her, the crickets, owls, and bullfrogs sang. Every creature seemed louder than normal. Hiding seemed to increase every sound. Tempest looked up at the stars, then back to the woods. She was careful to keep her back to the fire. She knew it was a bad idea to wreck her night vision by looking into the fire.

Dawn slowly approached, the sky slowly started to brighten. Oranges and pinks, then turning bright red. A storm was coming. Tempest went into the hut, waking Laura. She motioned for her to follow her outside. "OK Laura, I need you to go to Emor. Tell Sarge everything, then send word to Raven. See if they can pick us up. You heard Rebel, we can't move Scott for a few days. We need her to know we disabled the teleport device, don't tell them it was Scott. He's been through enough."

Laura nodded, "yes, they might pin collaboration on him or something." She fetched her bag from the hut, then running, she vanished into the woods.

Rebel woke soon after to the smells of cooking rabbit stew. Tempest had found dried herbs and some vegetables being preserved in another hut. Rebel stretched as he came out, picking up a bowl, groggily. "Sleep well?" She asked he only nodded, "how's Scott, really?"

Rebel let out a sigh, "the wounds, themselves, will heal fine but the infection is another matter. Tempest, he was hardly kept in sanitary conditions. If he wasn't so young and a werewolf, he would already be dead. He's running a high fever. He needs a healer from AMS, not a flight medic like me. I just hope help comes in time. I assume that's where you sent Laura. He's sick and I can only do so much."

"Try to keep liquids going down. We have to keep his strength up somehow. Let me know if I can help. I'm going to cook, clean and keep watch until you need me." She stirred the soup.

Rebel nodded, taking two bowls of soup back in the hut with him. She got up, checking the huts to make sure everything was secure. Tempest started exploring around the outskirts, collecting fresh herbs and hopping to help Scott.

Rebel had Scott sitting up, outside the hut by the fire under several blankets, though he was still shivering and extremely pale. Tempest walked over, giving fresh herbs to Rebel, then sat next to Scott. "So teleportation?" She asked he simply nodded, "when did it start?"

He smiled weakly, "right after you guys fixed magic. I appeared where I had been running for. Poof, I was across the field. Jessica said to be quiet about it, not to tell anyone. Apparently, it's a gift that hasn't been seen since the war. When the last teleporter teleported a virus into the headquarters of the vampires. Teleportation only manifests if there is great need." His voice barely above a whisper, his teeth chattering.

She nodded and looked at Rebel who shook his head. He motioned for her to follow him. She got up and they walked a little ways away. "Day, day in a half if were lucky, but he needs a healer. The infections spreading faster than I can combat." He admitted and she simply nodded. He went back to Scott, helping him inside to lay down. Tempest climbed a tree, watching for Atlantis. She knew all the gryphons were hunting Orben. The bats were patrolling the boarders and the dragons were traveling the towns, warning people. Their hope lay with a floating city. She reminded herself, that she had helped disable the engine.

CHAPTER 36

HELP ARRIVES

A DAY PASSED, WHEN SHE HEARD A rustling in the underbrush. Out of the bushes emerged Laura and Rain. Laura didn't wait, turning, she headed back to the city. Rain, however, went into the hut. Tempest didn't go in. She knew Rain and Rebel had a job ahead of them. Instead, she cooked more stew, keeping watch. Every couple of hours, she closed her eyes to rest, never sleeping for long.

Dusk came and went, the night fell and still she waited. Just as the dawn sun rose, Rebel came out and threw up, followed by Rain. Both looked exhausted. Rain sat down next to Tempest and grinned wearily. Her eyes betraying her age. "We purged his blood. Rebel did quite well keeping him alive. He will have his classes changed to medic training at AMS, when things settle down." Tempest smiled, she knew he would be happy and his father would be furious. "Scott will be protected. The werewolves will be notified he has been found. Jason was informed that you took out the teleport device. Vlad and Jason are now leading the sweeps. We will find Orben."

Tempest added wood to the fire, "when will Scott be well enough to travel?" She asked glancing at the hut.

Rain only smiled, "when he wakes, he should be right as rain."

She nodded glad to hear he would be fine. Rebel sat down, heavily, looking proud of himself. "You kids should not have gone into Orben's ship alone. That was foolish. I won't argue though, you did good work. Rebel told me about Scott being the telaporter." Tempest glared at Rebel. "Do not be mad at him. It was not his fault. When doing intensive healing, our minds were completely open."

Rebel nodded, "Tempest, your grandmother is going to keep it a secret, right?" He asked looking to Rain who nodded.

"It is wise to keep it a secret. He's a kid and a teleporter. Teleporters were often abused for their gifts," her grandmother told her. She nodded and looked towards the door as it creaked. Scott came out of the hut. He glowed with health, smiling brightly. "Thanks for saving my life," he told Tempest. He sat down, taking a bowl of soup and drinking it, not bothering with the spoon.

"Rebel and my grandmother saved your life. I simply rescued you from Orben." Tempest held out a bottle of water for Scott. He took it, drinking deeply.

Rain looked at Scott, "I think we should get you back to Rhydian. Perhaps we can send you to his people. Laura could escort you. As I recall, he has some family your age Scott." She smiled at him, "Gidget and Gadget, they are quite the geniuses. They are good kids."

Scott looked concerned, "I thought the chameleon people were reclusive, a closed community."

She nodded, "they are. They only let in a few outsiders, every couple of years. Though I am certain, Rhydian can arrange you passage with Laura, or take you there himself. At least there, you would be safe, until Orben is caught. Then we can get you back to your pack. With him on the loose, it's not safe for you." She looked to Rebel and Tempest. "You two should return to Emor with us, though I doubt you will heed my advice."

Tempest only smiled mischievously, "you are correct. I plan to stop Orben and Telemont."

Her grandmother nodded, "I would expect nothing less from my grand-daughter. One hour, then we break camp. Be gone by then, or I'll have no choice but to take you back with me." The pair nodded. They stood together, gathering what they would needed for the hunt. They were going to be trav-eling on foot, undetectable. They wanted to avoid the other hunters, who would be looking for Orben. They were considered in training, thus they should have taken her grandmothers instructions as orders. They should be going with her, staying safe, out of the way. Tempest looked at her grand-mother, "you don't have to ask, I'll keep Scott safe." Rain said smiling.

Scott grimaced at the idea of being looked after. "I think he was heading for a weapon stash. An old one, something before the war, located in the rainforest."

She nodded, "Tempest, Rebel that sounds like the Echo caves, deep in the mazes. There is a weapon stash, old weapons that are forbidden. They are capable of wiping people out, mass extinction weapons. The caves are a maze, designed to keep people out." She told them.

Rebel nodded "would it be possible to get a map of the caves? I know the way to the caves. They are located in the rainforest of my home." He was smiling, rubbing his hands together. "I can run as fast as wolves. Two weeks of travel." He took the bags, disappearing into the woods.

Rain took a piece of paper from her bag, writing directions on it. She handed it to Tempest. "After you use these directions, destroy them." Tempest nodded as she glanced over them. Rights, lefts, no turns, back tracks all written to get them safely through the Echo caves. Rebel appeared near the tree line, waiting for Tempest. She looked back at Rain. She shook her head, "don't you dare say goodbye or I may have to drag you back to the city."

"I'm going to go, umm, find firewood." She told Rain, who nodded. "See you later."

"Good luck, avoid splinters." Rain told her as Tempest got up, going to join Rebel in the woods.

CHAPTER 37

⁎

LAST CAMP

THE PAIR DISAPPEARED INTO THE FOREST. As they lost sight of the village, Rebel picked up a pair of bags he'd dropped earlier. They put the bags on and started jogging through the trees.

"The Echo caves are in the rain forests. Flyers aren't allowed in the rainforest of my people. They will have to land in the tree top city, and my people will send their own force down to investigate." Tempest nodded as they continued jogging. They didn't stop for the night and barely paused to eat. When they did stop to eat, he made an herbal drink that kept them wired and awake. Far more powerful than caffeine. They kept running for several days, stopping and napping occasionally. Two weeks later, they arrived at his rainforest. They stopped at the edge for the night, making camp at the edge of his home.

"From here on, don't eat any plants without checking it with me. Walk where I walk, do what I do." He instructed, looking at the trees. He didn't look worried, just confident.

She touched his arm, "I'll be careful and do as you ask. These are your lands, you were well behaved in mine, I will do the same."

He nodded, "I'll take first watch, if you make supper." She grinned and got to work on supper. They had figured out rather quickly, if they wanted food that tasted good, Tempest cooked. If they wanted food to sustain them, Rebel cooked. Tempest cooked a rabbit Rebel had caught earlier. She knew when she went to sleep, he would make the remains into a stew. Rebel set up the tent and unrolled a sleeping bag.

"We sleep in the tent, everything in the forest has adapted to kill. The wolves challenges are nothing compared to my land." He looked up at the trees towering behind her. Tempest nodded her understanding, "there are blood eating trees. Spiders the size of a pinhead that can kill in seconds and, of course, the poisonous plants."

They ate quietly, with him staring longingly at the trees. "I had to stay up in the treetops, until I had learned all the ways of nature and passed my tests. We rarely allow outsiders to learn our ways. We have our own governments and our own way of policing. Rhydian's people are from these forests, as well as a host of other species. His people have long since moved on, to more secretive places."

"Is there a name that encompasses all of these people?"

He nodded his head laughing. "You mean Jason hasn't told you?" She shook her head. "Anaman is the title used for us all. You have the subspecies, some of whom you've met. Jason's people are werewolves obviously, while my own are Fossasions, Laura's are Tigresses. Vlad's people are vampires as you know."

Tempest looked to the stars, they were different from her own. "My parents must be getting worried," she said quietly. Concern was written across her face. "I've been gone for three weeks now. Steve must be going out of his mind."

Rebel nodded, "are you afraid what happened to your great grandmother will happen to you?" He watched her for the first time since they'd gotten to the edge of the rainforest.

"Goodnight Rebel," she said, ending the conversation and ignoring his question. She finished eating and climbed into the tent. The truth was, she was terrified of becoming her grandmother. Vanishing from the human world without a trace, leaving her family. Tempest lay there, eventually falling into a dreamless sleep.

Hours later, Rebel woke her for her turn to keep watch. He slept and Tempest sat, staring into the dark trees that made up the rainforest. She could not help but feel as though eyes were watching her, though she could see none.

CHAPTER 38

INTO THE RAINFOREST

WHEN DAWN ARRIVED, TEMPEST WOKE REBEL. They broke camp, setting off into the trees. There was less sunlight penetrating the forest floor. As they walked, the air became more moist and the ground was softer. The trees were so large around, not even ten people could encircle them. They walked deeper, until they reached a hole in the ground. It looked like an abandoned mine shaft. Rebel paused for a moment, looking around. He pointed up, "I'll be right back, don't move." He jumped up a tree nearby, leaping up the branches. Moments later, he came falling down the tree. He landed in front of her. "Orben's ship is approaching from the north, what do you want to do?" He asked as he picked up his bag from the ground. "We've got ten minutes give or take."

Tempest looked at the mine shaft, "can you see in the dark?"

He chuckled, "do man eating trees eat meat?" Tempest took that to mean yes.

"Okay, follow my lead." Tempest took the directions out of her pocket. She read them aloud, following the directions as they went down. They could barely see the opening. Tempest slid her visor down, which let her see in the dark. They watched as people started coming down behind them.

They heard Orben calling out orders, "spread out. Find the weapons cache, then report to me. Touch nothing! Remember if you get your self in a trap we will not be rescuing you!."

Tempest turned to Rebel. "Whoever comes around the corner, we kill." He nodded, his nails lengthening to become claws.

"You sure?" He asked, she nodded, they stood waiting. Around the corner ran a repto. Rebel swiped his hand out, catching the repto at the throat. He flipped, falling backwards. Rebel leapt on him, using the lizards tail to tie his hands behind his back. Rebel looked up at Tempest grinning, "I'm not a fan of killing," he admitted sheepishly.

She nodded, "ok you tie them up I'll move them. How many do you figure before Orben comes down?" He simply shrugged, as she moved the next repto out of his way. Rebel took care of another pair. Then the hall blacked out. Rebel grabbed her arm, pulling them deeper into the caves.

CHAPTER 39

UNEXPECTED CAPTURE

T HE AIR FELT LIKE IT WAS turning to ice in their lungs. Tempest heard Rebel gasp beside her. "So, we have visitors. Orben would you like to show our guests to the ship?" Telemont said, his voice like ice. "My pleasure," Orben said. The darkness wrapped around them, becoming a physical presence. Suddenly, the cave flared with light. People rushed in, they were dressed in the deep greens of the trees above. Quickly, they surrounded Orben and Telemont.

"Time to go, Orben" Telemont said as they vanished into their own shadows. The reptos melted into their shadows and were gone as well.

Rebel took a step forward, to the people. "Rebel!" Came a sharp female voice, "what the name of all things green are you doing here!"

"I-" He started to say.

"No, you know these caves are off limits, we had a plan! A trap. We would have had them, if it weren't for you being down here!" She walked forwards into the light. She was like Rebel and his father Sarge, the rounded ears, the lightly fur covered face. Rebel scowled, "hello Sarah, good to see you too." He said pulling Tempest forward, "this is Tempest. Tempest, this is the leader of the Fossasions, my sister Sarah."

They were lead out of the tunnels, back to the rainforest floor. "Samuel, go tell the guards of Emor: Telemont and Orben have escaped." She held out a hand to Tempest. "It is an honour to meet the human who helped save magic, but if you two could please accompany me, to the edge of our forests. We will send you on your way."

Tempest shook her hand, and nodded "I realize you don't like us in your home forests, but we have a job to do. We will leave as quickly as possible."

"She's right Sarah, we're tracking Orben, Tempest has a score to settle with Orben for being such a pain." Rebel explained. He looked at Tempest, "we've a job to do."

Sarah shook her head, "all the more reason for you 'kids' to return to Emor." Tempest looked at Rebel and shrugged.

"Guess we've got no choice." Rebel grinned showing his sharp teeth.

"Oh no Rebel, I know that look." Sarah shook her head. "You two had better come with me."

"What?" He innocently asked grinning. Sarah gently cuffed him around the ears.

"I know when my baby brother is planning to go against my orders. You and Tempest will come and stay in the tree top city, until we can arrange transport back to Emor." She told them. "Spread out, guard the forest. If you see the ship, send word to the city. I doubt we will see him darken our forests again." Her troop disappeared soundlessly, into the forest. She lead the pair deeper into the dark woods. Tempest and Rebel followed closely, past the trees and fauna. They reached a group of tall ancient trees, when Sarah looked at Rebel. "You first, go kick the basket down."

Rebel launched himself at one of the trees, going straight up the rough bark. A few moments later, a basket descended from the canopy above. "Get in Tempest," Sarah instructed. Sarah pulled the rope attached to the basket which started to slowly ascend. Sarah ran up another tree nearby, gravity seemed to lack a hold on Fossasions.

CHAPTER 40

TREETOP CITY

W HEN TEMPEST FINALLY EMERGED FROM THE lower canopy, she saw a whole different world. There were homes built into the tree trunks, and hammocks slung about. Everyone seemed to be busy. Some were working out, others were sharpening weapons and some were building weapons. It appeared very militaristic. Rebel helped Tempest from the basket as she stared around herself. Sarah nodded her satisfaction. "Come now no dawdling you can bunk in the guest house." She lead them past the workers, who barely looked up at her as she passed. Sarah lead them to a doorway in a tree, which revealed that the tree had been hollowed out. Within, there was a pair of bunk beds carved into the walls. "You will remain here until we have time to escort you out of our rainforest." She turned to Rebel, "you should not have returned." Sarah turned and left.

Over the door tree bark spread, closing the door off from them. Tempest looked over to Rebel, "don't ask." He said before laying down on one of the beds. She sat down beside him.

"No luck, you're part of my team, so your going to tell me what is going on." She demanded, he turned to her.

"When I chose to go to Emor, to become a flyer to join the guard, I accepted exile from here, as did my father. We turned our backs on our people." He admitted looking at the wall where the door had been. "Sarah hates us for it. Our mother and her are like the amazonian women of old, it is how our people function. The men take the lower ranks, the women are the leaders," he admitted before turning his back on the room.

Tempest went to the other bed and lay down. She closed her eyes, sleeping for hours. Suddenly, her mind erupted in pain. She let out a groan, sitting up, her head in her hands. She saw her city, her home. It was under attack and fire rained from above. The whole city had fire lighting the streets. Tempest shook her head and looked at Rebel. "My home it's being…destroyed." She whispered feeling sick. "I have to get back!" Her mind was filled with comet like fireballs bombarding her city.

Rebel went to the doorway, banging on it, trying to get it open. As soon as it did open, Tempest pushed past Sarah and Rebel. The guards of Emor were still mounting up, Tempest didn't ask she leaped onto a gryphon. She took the map from her pocket and requested to be taken back to the human world. They flew to her world, night and day they flew onwards. When they finally reached the edge of the magic world, she saw the park. The trees were burnt, the playground destroyed and cars turned to hulking wrecks.

On the hill top stood her brother Steve, standing, waiting for her. He waved towards her and she landed on the hill by him. She jumped off, hugging him. "What happened Steve?" His arm still around her, holding her tight.

Steve held her at arms length. "Tempest, these storms came out of no where, the sky was filled with fireballs. They rained all over the world at virtually the same time. The world governments have issued martial law, in most countries. Our own city has a curfew, which reminds me, we need to get out of here and get to the shelter, as fast as possible." He looked at the gryphon, he touched the beak, "go home friend." He whispered and the gryphon took off. He looked at Tempest, "we need to go before we are caught." Steve told her as they jogged out of the park. The city had seen it's own devastation. There were fireball craters and fires still burning in other areas. Steve took Tempest through the city, to a local school. "We're staying here, do as I tell you."

CHAPTER 41

SHELTER

"WHAT HAPPENED TO OUR HOUSE?" SHE looked around her city. Power flickered and the cars were crashed in a multitude of places.

"It's still there, but everyone has been rounded up into the schools. There is no electricity and fires still burn." As they walked in, he went to a desk set up by the door. "Steve Storm, returning from clean up detail with another survivor." He told the receptionist who sat behind the desk.

She used an emergency laptop, typing his name in. "Why are you so late Steve and who do you have with you?" The woman asked watching them.

"A survivor, my sister. Rain Storm is her name on her birth certificate but we call her Tempest. I found her in the mall sector." He held her tightly to his side.

"Nowhere near the forests?" She asked watching him he shook his head.

"No ma'am, my sister's a mall rat through and through." He pulled a badge out. "She is my little sister and as human as I am." Tempest watched curiously.

"She'll still have to endure the testing. After that, she can have her badge and her work assignment. Until then, you know what must be done. Or must I call an escort?"

Steve shook his head, "no, I'll take her up to the testing area." He gripped her upper arm as he took her up to the second floor.

CHAPTER 42

PASS OR FAIL

" DO NOT USE MAGIC, WHATEVER YOU do. Focus on a completely human memory, a day in class or something simple." He told her taking her into a classroom, devoid of all but one chair. "Sit." He told her, "I'll be right here." He went to stand next to the door.

"What is going on?" She was confused as she sat on the chair waiting. She looked around the room, "what's happened Steve?"

He sighed, "they must test you for magic. If you have it, you are imprisoned. They know magic is behind the attack. Those with magic, are taken away to camps." He said slowly. The door opened and a man in a military uniform walked into the room.

"Steven, you do not have to stay for this." He said looking at Steve, "she is your sister as I understand it and as you know this is far from a pleasant test."

"That is why I must stay Logan, sir, she is my family, all I have left. Our parent's are still missing or have been taken." Steve said straightening up and walking forward, "it is unknown."

The military man nodded, looking at Tempest carefully. "You are sure she is human, Steven?" He only nodded remaining silent, "then we shall use the easiest test. Secure her," he walked out into the hallway.

Steve looked at Tempest, "whatever happens, you will be alright just concentrate. Don't use your magic Tempest." He instructed, he came forward, tying her arms to the chair arms. He tightened the ropes, holding her in place as Logan walked back in.

He looked at Steve, "do you want to do the honours then?"

Steve nodded, "yes sir," he looked at his sister. The man nodded and pointed at a machine in the corner. It resembled an eye exam machine. Steve brought it over, wheeling it in front of her. He positioned it over her eyes.

Logan undid her right hand, holding her arm tightly. A burning pain shot through her arm. Memories flooded through her, of the trials, of her adventures, in the other world and of saving her friends. She felt her magic starting to kick in, trying to heal her. She closed her eyes and the pain worsened. "Open your eyes, kid," Logan spoke and she shook her head trying to get away from the burning pain in her arm. She focused in on a safe childhood memory, playing with Steve in their treehouse. She opened her eyes, allowing her eyes to be scanned.

A few minutes later, the pain subsided and the machine beeped, spitting out a card of paper. "Human," Logan announced. "Steven don't forget to get rescanned this week. Give her the rundown and keep her away from the hotspots. Get her a badge pass too." He ordered before leaving the room.

Steve untied Tempest, "come on Tempest," he said softly. Tempest got up, rubbing her arm where it had been burned with what she now saw was a candle.

CHAPTER 43

NEW WORLD

S TEVE LEAD HER UP SEVERAL STORIES, to the top of the school. They stood up on the roof, surveying the world around them. Many blocks around them were burned out. As the sun set, several places began go glow, pulsing bright green, like magic. "Those are the hotspots. Most are or in the process of being quarantined. You must stay away from those. The magic in those places is capable of contaminating the human gene like radiation, anyone contaminated is taken away. Stay in the fenced area, around the school." He lead her back down the stairs, to the receptionist. "I'd like to collect a badge for Tempest Cloud. Commander Logan said she is human." He handed over the card that the machine had spat out.

The receptionist nodded and had Tempest stand against the wall, where she took her picture. "You are rescanned every seven days, if you work outside or stray from the yard. The test changes, often. If you do not work outside you are rescanned every fourteen days. You are in the girls dorm, in gym A. Meals are served three times a day, in the cafeteria. Your card gives you access to both, along with the yard."

Tempest shivered, her friends would never last here. They would be found out in an instant. The receptionist sat back down at her desk, printing the card. She handed it to Tempest, "follow the rules and you will be fine." Then she turned to look at Steve, "are you still interested in the strike back effort?" Steve nodded and held out his card. She swiped through the computer then handed it back. "First meeting is tomorrow morning, in the teachers lounge." She told him, "be careful Steven." He smiled taking her hand and kissing it.

"Of course, Cherie." He then lead his sister down through the halls to the gyms. "That's gym A, the girls dorm." He pointed to a sign on the door. "I'll be next door, in the guys side. Go on, your badge gets you a bed." He softly patted her back. She nodded and walked through the door. She scanned her card in the reader. The door swung open, revealing a room filled with women, milling about and talking.

"Find an empty bed and write your name on the paper at the foot." Said one grey haired woman. Tempest wandered around until she found a bed. She wrote her name on the blank sheet of paper. Once that was done she stuffed a small bag under her bed then she lay down and immediately fell into a deep sleep.

CHAPTER 44

STEVE'S MISSION

IN THE MORNING, STEVE ROLLED OUT of bed and got dressed in jeans and a T-shirt. He then went to the teachers lounge. He put his card through the reader and the door popped open, giving him access. He walked in and stood at the back of a large group of men. Logan stood at the front, talking. "These attacks happened all over the world. As such, our military is stretched to the breaking point. We are forced to hire civilians to help. Now, we don't have time to train you. That means, learn as you go or be sent back here to help the women, children and the old. We need two teams. One will be building walls around our city, separating us from the plague. The second team will be going into the danger areas to ferret out our attackers. Bring them back alive or dead, they are terrorists. My superiors believe it is a small settlement in the woods, on the edge of town. Everyone will undergo level five scans before leaving, and upon their return. Now, wall builders step forward, receive your badge updates. Anyone for armed attacks, follow me out back. We will see how you are with firearms and swords, though we doubt firearms will work there. Everyone else dismissed." Logan walked from the room.

Steve walked out, following Logan, with a group of others. Laid out in the back field, were a variety of weapons stations. Logan stood in the centre, waiting as the small group formed. One station was guns, another archery, sword fighting and even dagger fighting. "Alright, this is simple. We want to see what you civilians are good with, then we assign you to a job." Logan directed people to separate to the stations.

Steve tried first the guns, then sword fighting. Neither seemed to suit him. He walked to the dagger fighting area, where he proved to be proficient. Archery was up next. If he was going to be on a team, it would have to be here. If not, he wouldn't be able to get into the magic world, to contact the Anaman and warn them. He shook his head, glancing up at the school. He knew once his sister found out what was going on, there would be no way he could prevent her from going back. Looking around himself, he checked to make sure no one was watching him too closely. Steve blinked and his eyes flashed a brilliant orange, as he lined the bow with the furthest target. He let the arrow loose, flying true it twanged as it hit the centre of the bullseye.

A hand dropped onto his shoulder, "good shot Steve." He heard, turning to look at Logan. "Do it again and you're on the team. We need to know it wasn't a fluke." Steve nodded, carful to turn away from Logan. He loosed a second arrow and it flew as true as the first, splitting the first arrow with a satisfying thunk. When he turned back around to Logan, the man was watching him strangely. "Are you sure you want to risk your life, now that you have your sister here?" He took the bow and lead Steve towards a card scanner that was set up at the school wall.

He hid his smile, "it is for her that I do this." He answered, "to protect her and others like her."

Logan took his card, sending it through the reader. "This will authorize you a bow from the armoury. Find one that suits you and swipe your card to key it to you. Next time I see you, I expect you in uniform. We leave at dawn, be ready." He warned walking to the sword area.

CHAPTER 45

ARMING UP

STEVE WALKED TO THE MAKESHIFT ARMOURY. It was a tractor trailer that had been dropped off. He walked up the stairs, swiping his card in the reader. The door clicked open and a light flicked on above. The walls were lined with weapons, each secured in place behind chain link fencing. He walked along the wall, finding a compound bow and quiver. The fifteen arrows lay within, with a list of cleaning directions and a note saying he was responsible for his arrows cleaning, repair and replacement.

Next he went inside to the receptionist. "Hello, do you know where a handsome young man can find the uniform boxes?" He smiled as he had the bow and quiver over his shoulder.

She smiled back, "of course, though I only see a scruffy boy before me. Shall we see if theres a man under that scruffy hair cut?" She chuckled. Standing up, she unlocked the door behind her. Steve followed her in to the room, "what are you six, ten?" She asked as she hunted through a box of uniforms. He nodded, going to a dog tag machine. He made himself a set of ID as she found him a uniform. "Make sure you shave and cut your hair." She instructed as she handed him the uniform. He nodded as he went down to the mens room. He cut his hair and shaved, then he changed to his uniform: olive cargo pants, olive t-shirt. He then went to find his sister.

CHAPTER 46

ANSWERS GIVEN

T EMPEST STOOD ON THE ROOF STARING off towards the woods, the map card clutched in her hand. Her paw print glowed bright green, her blue grey eyes mixed with green. "Steve, what exactly is going on here? What was that test and why did you say I was a mall rat?" She turned to stare at him, "how do you know of the magic world and the Anaman anyway?"

He sat on the edge of the roof, motioning for her to join him. "Telemont's an old enemy he's been tormenting the world for hundreds of years. Orben is a menace and his newest sidekick. The best I can figure, Telemont got an attack past the guards of Emor. The test is to make sure you are entirely human. I know how to fool it, as you saw. A war is brewing and I know of no way to stop it from here. I am going to try to contact my friends, on the other side. See if I can get them to help. You need to stay here, safe. Keep to the mall rat story, it will help. I know of the magic world, I had my own adventures there. Remember when I went to camp?" She nodded patiently, "well, I found my way to the Anaman magic world. Where you went through the park to the wolves, I went through to the hawks. To Talon and his flock of Sky Dancers." He told, her his hand going to his shirt collar. He pulled it to one side, revealing a black tattoo of a birds silhouette, his eyes blazed bright orange. "It'll be alright Tempest, just stay here," he instructed. Taking her hand, he helped her up and back into the school, leading her down to the gyms.

The next morning, Steve and a small strike team left for the woods. The wall builders left. The plan was to build a great wall around the city, to keep out the unwanted contaminants. A few days later, Steve and the others returned. They were immediately taken up to the top floor, where screams were heard for five hours straight. Tempest stood waiting, at the back stairwell. When Steve finally came down, he looked like death warmed over. He shook his head as he walked past her. She followed him outside, to the field "Tempest you need to pack your bag now. Get ready to leave at lights out." She nodded not speaking, "don't make it obvious-"

She stopped him, "I still keep a bug out bag packed. Don't worry, security here is a joke. Getting out isn't an issue."

He nodded, "ok, two hours after lights out we go." She nodded and went into the school, checking that her bug out bag was ready. Then she laid on her bed, pretending to be fast asleep, waiting. When the time came to leave, Tempest snuck out, meeting her brother at the front door. They moved through the city remaining undetected, until they were halfway through. They heard car engines and spot lights swept over them. That was it they were spotted by a roaming patrols.

"Stop or we'll shoot!" Yelled a man in a patrol jeep. Tempest and Steve turned down an ally, only to run into another patrol. Steve grabbed Tempest by the shoulders, lifting her into the air, as huge wings sprang from his back. He flew them over the city to Firemen's park.

CHAPTER 47

ANOTHER ENTRANCE

"THERE'S A PORTAL HERE?" SHE ASKED looking around them uncertainly.

Steve nodded, "in all natural areas there is a way to true magic. There are many ways into the magic world, you must simply know where to look."

Tempest nodded, seeing her brother in a new light. He lead her through the park, to a grove of trees. "Nice wings." She said as he folded them back to his back, vanishing.

Steve nodded, "a gift from my friends." He walked into the grove. Standing in the centre, he looked at her. "All aboard who are coming aboard." She took his hand and he hugged her to his chest. "Under moonlight, centre of trees, cradled by the wind, take us home." He said loudly. Instantly, the wind picked up, spinning around them, then lifting them up. They were bathed in moonlight, the light reached blinding levels. When Tempest could see again, she saw they stood on a cliff top. So high up, that below lay a sea of clouds, rolling like the waves of an ocean. The stars that hung above them, burned brighter than any she had ever seen.

Steve grinned, "home at last." He smiled, though all Tempest could see was rocks and clouds. "Ready for a climb?" He asked her, as he pulled a rope from his bag. He tied one end around his waist and the other around hers.

She nodded, "yea, I guess but why not just fly down?"

"I'm out of practice and the air currents here make it dangerous for all but the best flyers, and the Air Knights." He held the rope as Tempest lowered herself over the edge, and down the cliff face. They climbed down the wall, carefully until they reached the cloud deck. Tempest's feet hit the stone ledge first and she helped Steve set his feet on it. He lead her along the ledge, until they reached a tunnel entrance.

CHAPTER 48

SINKHOLE CITY

T HEY WALKED, SIDE BY SIDE, INTO the tunnel. The tunnel narrowed and slopped as they walked. As they reached the end, a light appeared, daylight. They emerged in a large cavern, "welcome to Sinkhole City, the training centre of the Sky knights. The city was once on the surface but when the ground fell away, they moved." The city buildings were that of the desert, smooth sandstone abodes. The sky above was bright blue, with the sun just rising, bathing everything in light. The people were winged and had bright orange eyes. The wings were of every colour, from ever type of bird.

"Hey Sam!" Steve called to a woman, waving. She had a brown hair and orange eyes. She walked over, her wings were a light brown. She wore leather amour. A sword lay at one hip, a quiver and bow on the other.

"Hello Steven, how are you holding up? We heard of the last attack on your world. We have been gathering relief supplies." She said as she walked to them, "weird seeing you in regular clothes. Your room's still in the sleeping caves."

He looked down at himself and chuckled, "yes I'll get changed in a moment. First, I'd like to introduce my sister Tempest. Tempest this is Samantha. Sam for short. She flies for the Air Knights. We're ok, just exhausted. If your going to send relief supplies, be carful, my people are creating an army. Would you mind watching Tempest while I go get changed?"

She nodded, "sure, come on Tempest. You can tell me how you came by the magic world."

Tempest nodded, going to help Sam work on arrows. Her brother left to get changed. "Well, you see, I umm, I helped save the werewolves and magic."

Samantha looked surprised "you? But your such a small human." She looked up as Steve came back. He was dressed in leather gear, much like Sam's. A curved sword at his hip, his own wings folded to his back. His bow and quiver at his other hip.

CHAPTER 49

REUNITED

FOLLOWING HIM, HOWEVER, WERE THEIR PARENTS. They looked scared and human, unlike her brother his orange eyes glowing. Tempest ran to them, hugging them tightly. They spent several days together with the hawks, before Jason arrived. He took Tempest back to Emor with a contingent of Air Knights, including her brother and Samantha. It was time to find Telemont and Orben, no matter how long it took.

CPSIA information can be obtained at www.ICGtesting.com
Printed in the USA
LVOW12*2009211014

409854LV00002B/7/P